MOTHLIGHT

Also available from
Adam Scovell and Influx Press

How Pale the Winter Has Made Us (2020)

MOTHLIGHT

Adam Scovell

Influx Press
London

Published by Influx Press
49 Green Lanes, London, N16 9BU
www.influxpress.com / @InfluxPress
All rights reserved.
© Adam Scovell, 2019

First edition 2019.
Printed and bound in Great Britain by Clays Ltd, Elcograf S.p.A.
Paperback ISBN: 978-1-910312-37-7
Ebook ISBN: 978-1-910312-38-4

Editors: Dan Coxon and Gary Budden
Cover art and design: Vince Haig

For Nan

"...I feel as if I'm letting a ghost speak for me. Curiously, instead of playing myself, without knowing it, I let a ghost ventriloquise my words or play my role..."

— Jacques Derrida, *Ghost Dance* (1983)

1

To my knowledge, Phyllis Ewans had only two great preoccupations in her long life: walking and moths. An interest in these same two subjects also grew within me after a number of years of knowing her; such was the power of her influence. My predominate preoccupation today is with the study of Lepidoptera for my own academic research, and it was solely thanks to her that I followed this pathway. It dominates my life – that is, of course, when I am not plagued by my illness. Walking and moths had little to do with my early meetings with Phyllis Ewans, it must be said, and they certainly do not explain how I first came into contact with her. At that point in my childhood, Phyllis Ewans lived in the county of Cheshire, specifically The Wirral in the north-west of England. It is bordered by water: on one side the River Dee and the Welsh hills, on the other, the River Mersey and Merseyside. It was not until Phyllis Ewans moved down to London that I learned of her character and persona in more detail. However, being a fellow resident of Cheshire at the time, Phyllis Ewans and her sister Billie were loyal customers of my grandfather and his small business, selling them various household items regularly from his van.

On the day when I first met the sisters – a summer's day, which made sitting in my grandfather's van unbearable – Phyllis Ewans' house was the last stop. I remember the terraced house in which she lived, far from the grand London house in which I would later visit her. I never understood how the money was acquired to make such a change. 'She probably saved all the money she owed to your grandfather,' my grandmother once said, half-jokingly, sometime after the relationship between Phyllis Ewans and my own family had soured. The door of her house was green and had beautiful, stained-glass designs in the slats. The garden to the front of the house was, by comparison, ill-kept and littered with rubbish thrown by passing walkers. Phyllis Ewans, I remember, welcomed my grandfather into the thin hallway with hollow greetings. Much of the furnishing was incredibly old and a thin mist of dust and debris was always visible. I had never seen dust such as this before and quietly enjoyed disturbing it with my hand to create shapes and tiny whorls in the air. The walls were covered with mounted moths and, with hindsight, I imagine this dust to be an atmosphere of scales comprised of insect wings.

Such a structure on their wings is what gives rise to the very term Lepidoptera and Phyllis Ewans' hallway was a mausoleum of scales. I took little notice of her collection of moths at this point, more interested in the shelves of books, the incredibly patterned carpets and the assortment of ornaments and objects, all covered with a sheet of what looked like moth scales and dirt. I felt that I made little impression at the time, as was common when I met people. I was always a shy and inward-looking boy, as my grandmother had pointed out numerous times. But my lack of impression upon Phyllis Ewans was largely because of her sister Billie who, on the contrary, I made a swift impression upon, much to the surprise of my grandparents. Phyllis Ewans was far more discerning and could perceive at once my initial disinterest in being in their house. Billie, on the other hand, was delighted to have a young boy in their midst. She would coax me over to her chair next to the fire, and would do so many times hence. She was much older than her sister but had been a great mover in various social scenes earlier in life, as I would learn some time later from the many photographs I kept of her. These photos of Billie made me question the likelihood of the sisters actually being related at all, such was their difference in character and mentality. They were only sisters in name, and I still harbour daydreams surrounding the likelihood of their differing parentage.

Phyllis Ewans had time to spare in knowing me, whereas Billie's years were numbered. She still had the air of a great and fashionable lady, brought over from her youth which was one filled with expensive fur coats, pearls, jewels and silken stockings. Imagining Phyllis Ewans' undoubted scorn at such excess fills me with an amused delight now, considering the sly barbs I would encounter in my own conversations with her but applied to a more deserving victim. Having been coaxed over to the fireside, Billie reached for a small purse tucked under numerous layers of clothing and blankets. Her spindly fingers, no doubt thought of as delicate and desirable some forty years previous, wrapped themselves around a rolled-up note. She pulled my hand towards hers and, in front of the array of dead moths, placed the money in the palm of my small hand, gently wrapping my fingers around it with a ritualistic knowingness. This bought my attention for some time on that visit, during which I all but ignored Phyllis Evans. I was enraptured by Billie, who took great pleasure in touching the curls of my hair. As the veined and bony fingers ran their way over my head, I remember catching Phyllis Evans watching from the doorway with a look of a disdain that I would come to recognise later in life. This had clearly been the structure of their relationship for some time. Billie cared little for walking, and even less for moths. It is for this reason that I find her character intriguing, considering her sister was so driven by these subjects. Perhaps it was a reaction to such obsessions, yet it is clear that Billie, when not playing up for a variety of men, would occasionally try to take an interest in her sister's passions.

I may have paid little attention to the many wonderful specimens of Lepidoptera upon the walls of Phyllis Evans' house on that trip but one moth enraptured me even then, and has done ever since. In fact, this point may arguably mark the earliest beginning of my own interest in moths, the germination of the obsession to which I thought I would devote my whole life. Perhaps Phyllis Ewans planned this, knowing the transient nature of Billie's affections or, with even more hindsight, knowing the few years she had left to live. As my grandfather went to leave, Phyllis Ewans decided to show me a specimen she had hanging in the furthest part of the hallway. Seeing an opportunity to discuss her favourite subject, she took the mounted insect off the wall and began to tell of its history with great gusto and character, which I would not have suspected possible from the seemingly quiet and sullen woman.

The moth had stood out from the others due to its great size and its solitary mounting. The other moths, while undoubtedly beautiful, were mounted in groups of genus, family, place of capture, and sometimes even curated by the whims of the entomologist. This moth was alone, housed in a small frame on a creamy white background with the label 'Laothoepopuli' written in beautiful, wavy handwriting. It seemed to my young eyes even then to possess some secretive importance, some unique position ahead of all the other moths. I still have the moth, or at least the remains of it after I dropped it in shock one afternoon. With its large rounded head and grey body, even before my obsessions with Lepidoptera took hold, this moth caught my attention with ease. Phyllis Ewans could see the effect it had upon me and took pride in not needing money to buy my attention. It was a well-preserved example of a poplar hawk moth, so named due to its caterpillar's penchant for the leaves of poplar trees. Its wings looked designed by the architect of a hotel from the great years of travel, with two smaller front wings that curved as if they were dripping slowly away from the thorax and down towards the abdomen. Billie did not get up to bid farewell, though my grandfather bellowed a goodbye down the hallway, met with a feeble sound from the room. Phyllis Ewans saw us to the door, thanking my grandfather for the supplies he had dutifully brought in spite of the sisters still owing him a reasonable sum of money.

Payment was agreed for a later date and the next delivery was arranged, though I fail to remember much of the visit after seeing the moth. My mind was transfixed by the poplar hawk moth's wings and its great size; the vision of it implanted upon my retina and seeming to speak of strange memories which were not my own. Later in life, I walked many miles to a multitude of traps in the hope of capturing and studying such a moth, one that has become less and less common as the decades have gone by. Luckily, this was to be the first of many meetings with Phyllis Ewans as I grew up. Yet there were many complexities that arose before our friendship could develop properly, and before the great mysteries of her life would envelop my own; her own existence dissolved into the air like the scales of wings in a hallway of dead insects.

After our first meeting, I would occasionally accompany my grandfather to visit Phyllis and Billie Ewans. The latter would regularly repeat the ritual of drawing me closer to her fireside nest, locating the purse which lay in some unknown spot under her blankets, and crumpling heavily folded notes into my hand. I had, however, grown more interested in her sister. Beneath the walled mausoleum of mounted moths sat numerous bookcases filled with morbid books about murder. I enjoyed these volumes of detective and murder fiction, specifically for their dramatic and colourful covers. One in particular stands out, an old volume with a wasp of huge proportions bothering a much smaller plane on its cover. It was only some years later that I was disappointed to find that the novel was virtually devoid of enormously proportioned wasps. In fact, its whole plot revolved entirely around the very absence of a wasp.

Phyllis Ewans walked in on this particular visit and found her sister attempting to disrupt my own burgeoning interest in walking and moths with a collection of photos. 'You don't want to look at those old books about moths. Come here and let me show you these.' The occasions of my visits grew one summer, due to being taken care of by my grandmother. Paying a visit to Phyllis and Billie Ewans was a simple and relatively cheap way of providing entertainment for an hour or two. Soon, Billie would stop coaxing me over with her insipid fingers and cease her attempts to barter for my attention. Such was the draw of the moths and the multitude of books, even Phyllis Ewans herself would initially struggle to rouse me from my curiously quiet and obsessive studies of their possessions.

I am unfair to Billie in my memories, though I know that my feelings were shared by my grandmother, who eventually had to look after her when the woman became

ill with age. Going through many photographs that my
grandmother saved from the purge of Billie's existence,
conducted by her sister after she passed away, they showed
evidence that Billie had at least attempted some compromise.
In one photograph, she can be seen clearly in Phyllis Ewans'
favourite spot, in Snowdonia in North Wales, attempting to
befriend a local sheep; her hand reaching out with a
contradictory mixture of confidence and nervousness. On
the rear of the photograph, written in Phyllis Ewans'
beautiful handwriting, is written: 'Billie making friends
with the land.'

I began to ponder what she had meant by such a curious description: did she believe Billie to be inducted into her vision of the landscape simply through some interaction with a farm animal? Perhaps Phyllis Ewans had thought that such an action, so out of character on her sister's part, meant an inevitable leeway in her thinking, an absolution of the resentment towards the rural climes which so often played a vital role in the loneliness of research. But the lack of similar photos shows, to my mind, that this was a rare case, one born of 'a lack of men one weekend', as Phyllis Ewans sharply put it one day many years later. I learned that this resentment was part of a wider divide between the sisters, and it was something that I became aware of even when visiting as a child.

It was only after Billie's death that I would walk up to her bedroom and find her personality neatly contained within the confines of her single room in the house. The room was alien compared to the others. There were no mounted moths or moth-trapping equipment, no books about walking, no walking sticks and very little in the way of objects that showed an interest in anything her sister cared for. A huge wooden wardrobe with mirrored panels bulged with the immense weight and volume of the clothes housed within. The air had a mist that was perceivable in the white rays of sunlight drifting through the murky net curtains. But – and I considered this even then – the mist was not fragments of wings from decaying Lepidoptera, but the disturbed remnants of powdered make-up. In many ways, they were the scales of another deceased creature. I rarely entered

the room after she died, for my visits lessened as Phyllis
Ewans prepared to move house. Before this, my visits had
germinated great gaps of time in between, Billie's dwindling
life garnering a flicker-book effect, her body fading into the
air around her. My interest in her waned from visit to visit
but this, in hindsight, had always been dictated by seeing
such a life edited through the intonations of her sister.

Despite Phyllis Ewans travelling regularly for
conferences and in search of further specimens of moths
around Europe, most of the documented evidence suggests
that Billie did, in fact, travel more widely and more often
than her sister. This may have had something to do with
Phyllis Ewans' role in several academic departments
around the country, which must have curtailed her
opportunities to travel far and for pleasure. Billie, in almost
total contrast, worked several minor jobs in various retail
roles, including numerous make-up counters in department
stores. With this income and freedom, she evidently
travelled with an unusual voraciousness. I found a
particularly captivating picture of Billie taken in India
riding an elephant. In the picture, she seems rather regal
riding upon it, clearly attempting to remain composed
despite the animal obviously being riled and in the middle
of an undoubtedly loud roar. Neither of the sisters ever
discussed the details of Billie's trips, of course. Phyllis
Ewans would never in her life engage in such an activity,
never mind insist on a photograph documenting it; proudly
freezing the moment in time, ready to be displayed to
friends and relived infinitely. There was clearly some pride

in the photograph at any rate, as it was kept in its own special protective holder made of a luxurious cream card, since discoloured and frayed around the edges with age.

Perhaps Phyllis Ewans did indeed wish to travel more, especially outside of Europe, which she explored in some detail in the earlier years of her life. 'Billie may have travelled a great deal,' Phyllis opined to me with dismissive envy on one visit, 'but she saw very little overall, considering.'

My grandmother eventually became an unofficial carer for the older sister. Phyllis Ewans had neither the time nor the compulsion to look after her. Even when her work did not draw her out of the house and down to London on the train, she still barely acknowledged the presence of her gradually crumbling sister. It was during one of these much later visits that Billie mentioned something in passing that further ignited my interest in Phyllis Ewans, firing my curiosity. When she believed my grandparents to be busy organising food on a winter visit, she fixed a stare at her sister, who was reading a book defiantly in the adjacent wooden chair, and rasped with a strange melancholy, 'We're alone now and will die so but I'm sorry.' It was as if I was not in the room, like I had faded into the strangely florid patterns of the dated chair, watching this private moment between the sisters in secret. Phyllis Ewans would continually deny, even up until the day she herself died, that Billie in fact said anything of the sort during that evening. What had Billie done, I thought, that Phyllis Ewans considered so awful as to behave so coldly towards her? Even my grandmother, forever in my thoughts as my most patient relative, occasionally lost her patience with Phyllis Ewans and her coldness towards her sister. Such a detached demeanour took my naturally caring and affectionate grandmother by surprise.

One summer's day, I joined my grandmother on her daily
visit to check up on Billie and her dying body. On entering
the house, to which she had been given a key, she found
her having spilt a hot drink, her arm partly burnt. The pain
had caused her to faint and, though Phyllis Ewans denied
hearing any such commotion – she was apparently working
upstairs, sorting through a variety of garden tiger moths
caught in a local patch of woodland – my grandmother did
not for a moment believe her. I remember the vision of Billie's
slumped body and see it as the moment when she had all but
died. Her funeral a week or so later was merely a triviality,
despite Billie surviving for a few days after the accident. The
shock of this event, and the implication that Phyllis Ewans'
detachment verged on neglect, meant that my grandmother
would subsequently grow apart from her, and was incredibly
surprised some years later to find my own friendship with
her to be so all-encompassing and dramatically detailed.

My memories of Billie's funeral service are aptly
somewhat mixed. This is due in part to the frantic atmosphere
that her death in the hospital initially caused, especially to
my grandparents, both of whom were left to deal with the
technicalities of the death in spite of the deceased's sibling
still being alive. The gaps in this period were later filled in
by my grandmother who still harbours a great resentment
towards Phyllis Ewans. It was at this point that I made the
visit to her room mentioned earlier, due, rather naively, to
my grandmother insisting on fetching several changes of
clothes for her stay in hospital, knowing full well that she had
not long to live. One of the most surprising things I found in

her room was a single Polaroid of Billie and Phyllis Ewans standing side by side. At that time, I had never seen a photo of the sisters together, and I was even more surprised to find that the location of the photograph was somewhere rural. Phyllis Ewans had clearly persuaded her sister to accompany her once more on a walking trip in Wales sometime in the recent past.

The house in the photo, which I paid little attention to then, would later be recognised as a key location in her shadow life. Though the ambivalence was still perceivable in the pair, it was the closest I had come to seeing them happy together; a moment long since dead. Had this moment been savoured as evidence by Billie; that she had at least attempted to make amends with her sister? It played upon my mind, reminding me that I was still in the dark regarding what exactly her sister had to make amends for. I kept the photo, worried that once Phyllis Ewans began sorting out the room and the house, she would undoubtedly throw it away. Years later, my reasoning was proved correct when I confronted her with it. 'I have something to show you,' I remember saying in the large front room of her south London house. Seeing the photo, she exclaimed with some dismay, 'Oh you should have thrown that thing away.'

I was unsure whether she was referring to the photo or, in fact, the very trace of the memory. Her sister had tried to meet her halfway, walking with her despite her great discomfort. I wondered how long the trip had lasted, what the pair had discussed on the long meanders up the many Snowdonian hills and mountainsides – if they had walked at all, that is. Phyllis Ewans may have wanted to discard the memory but I was determined to keep it. It sat for many years with the mounted moths that I inherited from her, the moths taking precedence in the weeks after Phyllis Ewans died, when my obsession with the women verged on an illness: the illness of Miss Ewans, as I would later take to calling it. I made sure to keep the picture propped up alongside a mounting of some garden tigers that I had cleaned up, removing the layers of dirt and dust from the glass frame.

For a brief period after Billie died, visiting the house was distinctly uncomfortable, caused by a rift that grew quickly between Phyllis Ewans and my family. She did not bother to venture to the hospital to wish any sort of goodbye to her sister, and ignored my errand to her sister's room in search of nightwear; clothing for a ghost now venturing away from the land of its body. It could be said that she ignored what my visit to her sister's room implied, so I thought after I had collected the items. It should have emphasised that her sister was now close to dying, but it seemed to her simply another visitation, a rattling spirit causing mild disturbances in the next, empty room.

My grandmother and grandfather commented on the lack of empathy from Phyllis Ewans who, far from mourning by any publicly recognised standard, seemed almost stronger, as if a great weight had finally been lifted from her shoulders. My grandmother would often say, with a surprisingly out of character morbid humour, that she believed Phyllis Ewans had only called on the afternoon Billie had been injured because the sight of the unconscious body, sat gathering dust in the living room, had distracted her research. 'The bloody body was distracting her from her moths,' my grandmother had said.

I later learned that Phyllis Ewans had even planned a walking to trip to Snowdonia for that upcoming weekend, and had delegated even more of the logistics of her sister's death to others to be able to take it. I know for a fact that she did indeed do this, as I remember her disappearing at an inopportune time when my grandmother needed her for the various legal ramifications revolving around the death certificate and other memoranda. I began to wonder what history, then invisible to my eyes, had separated the sisters to such an alarming degree. This separation was almost a physical manifestation while the pair were alive, filling the rooms of their shared house like an invisible water, a silence drowning all notion of pleasantries. This invisible substance had now soured. When the sisters had clearly been through a disagreement, which was seemingly very often, entering the room where they sat felt like diving deep into a murky lake.

Returning from her trip to Snowdonia, Phyllis Ewans had found all the funeral arrangements organised, my grandmother having been forced to take it upon herself to locate the required documents in the house. After several hours of rummaging through bureaus filled with Lepidoptera journals, half-finished mounts – the contents of which had since heavily disintegrated – and various scraps of articles and essays, she found what she needed. It was as if the dead insects had been accumulated as a sort of entomological compost, an unconscious attempt to rot away the official existence and documents of her sister's life with malicious intent.

The casual return of Phyllis Ewans from her trip, her hands loaded with her mothing net and various bags jangling with jars, caused a great argument which ended in the final divide. My grandparents had agreed to meet her, albeit doing their best to produce a frosty reception. I remember very little about the conversation – which I was, unusually, allowed to be present for – as I was instantly hypnotised by the moths that Phyllis Ewans had caught, some of which were still alive and fluttering around in small glass jars. It was only upon the loud sound of a hand hitting the side of a chair that I was brought out of my mesmerised state. My grandfather had lost his patience and had hit the chair in frustration. Later on in London, when I became reacquainted with Phyllis Ewans, I would learn that she had initially assumed I would follow the lead of my grandparents and have little to do with her after the death of her sister. Whilst I also questioned her behaviour at the time, the curiosity that she aroused in me was of an increasingly insatiable character, and far greater in its need to be quenched than my need to keep in line with my grandparents. There are many days, even now, when I wish I had followed their lead, if only to avoid being trapped in this permanent purgatory where my curiosity eventually landed me.

The day of Billie's funeral was an oddly dry affair, very unlike the wet funerals dampened with rain in my imagination. I accompanied my grandparents, as it had taken a great deal of organising on their part. The funeral service was uncomfortable but the paper handout given included a rare colour picture of Billie, so it was worth suffering the discomfort. The picture was a strange inclusion, and I wondered who had chosen it. Logically, it was either my grandfather or my grandmother. Billie is typically overdressed in the photo and stood in a public house, wearing a faded green dress and her hair blond and curled.

The aspect that most struck me about the picture, however, was the strange hanging design in the background. At first it appeared, from the angle of the photograph, like a French chandelier constructed from leaves; but on closer inspection, it resembled what could only be described as a skein of moths fluttering behind her, tormenting with that constant papery sound of their wings. I am, in hindsight, projecting my reaction to such hordes of moths onto the photograph, even if they are clearly there in the photo. I wish I had seen the picture when Billie was alive, perhaps asking her what exactly the strange presence was. Maybe it was a simple design brought into the pub to add a sense of glamour. Today I can't help but shudder when seeing it.

The thought of such a skein of moths took a great hold over my senses at the funeral, and I remember imagining that same flock constantly and chaotically flying close behind my shoulders. This would be the first of many such occasions when what can only be described as an attack took hold of my senses and rendered me useless. The priest conducting the service spoke slowly and hypnotically as the coffin was lowered into the arid grave. My grandmother cried and I could hear her sobbing behind the fluttering, a cacophony gradually drowning out all the priest's words, lost in the endless wingbeat of a thousand moths.

When the congregation were invited to throw their handfuls of dirt upon the wooden box, I remember hallucinating further. The dirt dissolved into many moth wings and scales, and I felt increasingly faint as the grave seemed to fill before my eyes with grey and brown wings, the dust rising in great swirls as the fluttering sound grew to painful levels. It was only when my grandfather took hold of my shoulders that I can recall my eyes opening, my pain clearly sensed by him. Phyllis Ewans had walked off some time before I came back to reality, and I took a moment to regain my balance. Billie had been buried, whether under dead wings or soil, and I knew that I was to follow the trail of these wings after her sister; following blindly towards the light if only to uncover the reason for her character. This was the curiosity she had imbued in me with parasitic precision.

I failed to see Phyllis Ewans again for quite some time after this. I became a lonely teenager, interested only in things that could excuse such loneliness. These were namely an insistence on long walks in Wales at the weekend and an increasing interest in moths. It was not until I moved down to London some years later that I would re-establish contact with the woman, by which time my own interest in these things had burgeoned into an early career. I therefore tell of Phyllis Ewans' departure from Cheshire to the south London suburb where she would eventually live and die in hindsight, following my many questioning meetings with her and through the photographs she would leave me after her death. I could no longer rely on the testimony of my grandparents for accurate detail regarding her life.

On one occasion, some years later in Phyllis Ewans' London living room, I asked her whether she had felt anything at the death of her sister. She had seemed puzzled at first, and the moment became briefly awkward as I thought I had asked too obvious a question. Of course, a sister would mourn her sibling, I thought. But she was to prove my awkward worry in vain, for she simply rolled her eyes, half loosened by alcohol, and said that she would never forgive her. This was indeed a surprise; that there was a definite divide between them caused by something. I pleaded to be told what it was – perhaps she had obstructed her in some vital piece of entomological research – but the realisation that she had said too much quickly overpowered the effect of her drink and she retreated quietly into her social cocoon once more.

It became apparent after Billie's death that she, Phyllis Ewans, had created a mounting of her sister's memory as if it was simply another captured moth. I'm sure she would have approved of the metaphor, the act of capture, killing and mounting no doubt providing a pleasing fantasy for one who so seemingly detested her sister. This mounting was naturally not a real one, but a photographic one left for me to find. Many of the photos of Billie were salvaged by my grandmother, who made one final visit to the property before cutting off all ties with Phyllis Ewans. During this visit, so she would tell me when she passed the photographs on, Phyllis Ewans was out sorting, so she assumed, the numerous bureaucracies that come with an impending move to

a new house. My grandmother still had the key with
which she would let herself in when providing care for
Billie. She recalled looking for several mementos of the
deceased, worried that Phyllis Ewans would attempt to
wipe away every trace of the woman, finally letting her
existence crumble into the surrounding scales of moth
wings and abandoned chrysalises. I know now that
my grandmother was correct to intuit this, as Phyllis
Ewans would later tell me of either selling her sister's
possessions or merely throwing them out. 'A moth,
after all,' she would suggest, 'does not, through fits of
nostalgia, visit its discarded cocoon after it has flown.'

Of the photographs that Phyllis Ewans kept, Billie is
marked almost totally by her absence: landscapes,
houses, moths, pictures of rooms in her Cheshire house,
but next to none of her sister. Absence was key to her
photographic eye. She seems to have documented her
sister's room in great detail, but only to emphasise Billie's
death. I realised later what these photographs meant
when I finally recognised the dressing table in a picture.
Gone were the lavish, glamorous visions of this
preparatory area of beauty I had seen, now replaced by a
ghostly emptiness. The room seems ordinary in the
photo, perhaps only being gifted its subtle glamour
through the presence of its occupant; the illusion now
disintegrating with the person's body to reveal the truth
underneath, the skin under the powder that had finally
withered away. Even more apt is Phyllis Ewans herself,
who has managed a unique conjuring trick within the

picture, the flash of the camera masking her own reflection in the mirror. She was perhaps collecting evidence, forming one last impression of her sister through an avoidance of sorts.

Another photograph is equally as empty, showing the far side of the same room, the mirror in the wardrobe again deployed to exaggerate both the size of the room and its lack of occupant. In doing this, Phyllis Ewans forced the ghost into the space, capturing it within an image of itself to control the existence of its memory. It is yet another cruel aspect that I find so surprising having known of Phyllis Ewans' warm nature, though this may have also been because of our shared interests in walking and in moths, something which she did not share with her sister.

Sometime later, when sorting through the remains of Phyllis Ewans' possessions, a picture of Billie finally surfaced. It was to be the second colour photograph of the woman that I saw. Hidden in one of the lesser Lepidoptera publications of the time – more as a bookmark than a secret – the photograph fell out whilst I was sorting through the journals, deciding which to keep. The photograph was well preserved, far less faded than most of the objects of the same age in Phyllis Ewans' possession.

Billie looks pale but happy in the picture, typically glamorous as she arranges a huge vase of flowers. It would have made for a better funeral photo. Her hair is surprisingly darker than the platinum blond in all other photographs of her. I suspected briefly that it was the flowers that had led to the photograph being saved rather than as a memento of a sibling, but the absence of Billie from all other aspects of the London house showed it to be otherwise. Perhaps, so I thought at the time, it was quiet evidence that Phyllis Ewans thought of her sister with more than simply the malice I had seen her fall back into during reminiscences. I looked deeply into the photograph, contentment exuding from its purplish light and busy textures. She had let her sister back into her life briefly at the very last moment. But why had she been banished in the first place?

Phyllis Ewans did not last long in Cheshire, once the last shackles of her neglected duty to her sister had crumbled into the moth-wing dust. I only heard of her plans through the hearsay of my grandmother. Arranging a more intense work schedule with a university department in London, the capital was her next destination in which to further her own studies. 'The most difficult thing,' she would later tell me, purring over a favourite cup of whiskey-dashed tea, 'was making sure the specimens were transported without any damage. Simply taking them off the walls was a difficulty, the smallest shake and they would just disappear.'

I can vouch for the difficulty in moving such moths. When moving the remains of her collection after she died, I encountered the very same problem. With a somewhat ironic realisation, I found that walking and moths, while naturally pairing when the latter were alive, made for an incredibly stressful combination when the insects had been dead for some time. I remember the care and time I took with the singular mounted poplar hawk moth which sat at the head of the collection, in spite of it not being rare. Phyllis Ewans seemed defined in this insect, its moody wings dulled even further by her death but still mostly intact. The collection was haunted by this moth and I let it hang for quite some time afterwards. Its frame mysteriously hadn't aged at all, as if it had been regularly replaced and renewed, even cleaned. This latter aspect is the most important to note, as Phyllis Ewans did not clean anything.

I was impressed when looking around the new hallway and living room by just how many moths had survived their long journey down to London. As I sat one day in the new London living room, Phyllis Ewans began to show me photographs of the Cheshire house again, keen for me to relive certain childhood memories but very much rewriting the history of them, as if her sister had never even existed.

I remember discussing the poplar hawk moth, which she resisted acknowledging, but other aspects clearly lit some inward nostalgia. On this occasion, we exchanged memories: my grandparents' visits and my financially rewarding introduction to her and Billie, whom she eventually had to acknowledge because I had known her through her money. She pulled out one photograph from a drawer and showed it to me, the nostalgia coming full circle as it fixed the memory with a warm visual. 'This was the last photograph I took of the house before I moved here,' she said, almost with pride. It was of the hallway of the house on a sunny day, spring edging its way in. The light shone beautifully.

Yet something odd struck me. 'But Miss Ewans,' as I would take to calling her once her sister had died, 'there's furniture still in the hallway. Did you not move a good while after this?' I remember her pondering the question for a while, perhaps considering and mapping the time between the photograph and her final departure from the Cheshire house. 'Oh no,' she said, 'I left that very week.' With this, the matter was closed, the photograph put away and the conversation brought back to moths, even though the presence of furniture in the photo was unusual. As we filed through more and more prints of the insects, some recently caught specimens and other entomological paraphernalia, it occurred to me that these moths and I were really the only two things that she had brought with her from Cheshire to London, though I admittedly came much later and only by chance. I still accepted, however, in spite of the coincidences that brought us back together, that I was equally brought along with her when she moved. I imagined her taking that last photograph, capturing the moment of release from the responsibilities of sibling life, now replaced with what seemed to be a new-found freedom. It would be in this period that Miss Ewans would begin to relate her life to me with more openness and detail, all observed through the dual prisms of walking and moths.

2

It would be some years before I encountered Miss Ewans again, though the parasite of her interests bred and grew stronger within me after she had left for London. Her timely introduction into my life was at the pinpoint moment when, impressionable and unfinished, her passions seeped into my own with ease. It was at this point that I began to ghost her life, following in her footsteps: sometimes symbolically with my study of biology, and sometimes simply by walking far into the northern Welsh mountains just as she had. I had little clue which paths were the exact routes she had taken through Monmouthshire and the rocky, green hills around Snowdonia. She apparently would continue making these walks, albeit more briefly, even after having moved down south, not so much as an escape from London but as a remedy to the city's more trying elements. I never encountered her though.

In hindsight, I was upset that Miss Ewans had not taken the opportunity of these occasional trips back to North

Wales to call upon me while I was still living in Cheshire.
I was left to walk alone. My first walk around Snowdonia,
I remember well, took place on a solitary day sometime
in my seventeenth year, and I would have appreciated
her company. I wanted to see what Miss Ewans had seen
and spoken of so often, on her fleeting visits to Snowdon's
view over the valleys before heading back through to its
greener, more tree-lined pastures in search of moths. 'I
had always wanted to find an Ashworth's rustic,' she once
told me confidently, before admitting that the one in her
collection had been purchased off another entomologist
who lived near the town of Llangollen. Where this catcher
had caught the moth was never fully disclosed. The moth
proved elusive to my own net as well, and I had excited
visions of the day when I would eventually catch it, simply
to impress her.

I once considered the possibility, when finally living in
London, of venturing up to Betws-y-Coed with the latest
electric-bulb Robinson Trap, ready to power the black-
domed object from some portable battery for several hours
in the hope of catching some interesting specimens, perhaps
even an Ashworth's rustic. I never had the chance to make
the trip, and feel little need to now that Miss Ewans is dead,
for I inherited the Ashworth's rustic bought from the catcher
in Llangollen. It's a popular specimen for essays in most
journals and papers on the subject of extinction, due to the
publicity of its rapid decline in numbers. It is an insect that
symbolises a melancholic, quiet passing. I imagined the
rare moth living a similar life to Miss Ewans, solitary and

camouflaged on the limestone but standing out upon the slate. I admired the purchased moth many times after her death, the specimen being one of the very few I intended to keep for myself, but, as I said one day to a colleague in the department, it didn't seem quite right that Miss Ewans prized a moth that she did not catch herself.

'It's perfectly normal,' my colleague replied, though I knew he was ignorant of her character. She had clearly been distracted by something else around these hills that I could not, at this point in time, attune myself to. She would have been highly critical if, for example, I had prized a moth that was possible to catch in this country but had not, in fact, caught it myself. Many photographs of Miss Ewans exist from a variety of locations in and around this area, one example showing a hillside garden. I found the photo trite at first. 'Of course it is Wales,' she was whispering to me from the dead. 'There are daffodils,' she said. I did not recognise the area at all at first, but this was chiefly because my knowledge of the place was determined by the most clichéd of visits or seen through the distraction of trying to find new specimens.

I had gleaned the interests in walking and moths superficially from Miss Ewans, in the way that many do when young and impressionable, and so I took to the most obvious ways to express this interest by fumbling around in an amateurish manner, and with little success. This meant climbing to the top of Snowdon on a regular basis as an excuse for not catching many moths at all. It was, thinking back, not the best of areas for indulging in such interests

anyway. But, as I often said to myself later, those walks
provided the basis for a genuine and nuanced interest once
I was in possession of more skills and knowledge on the
subject. The walks then instead provided opportunities for
quiet contemplation.

The loneliness which had seemed to pervade Miss
Ewans' life was also transferred to my own, just as the
moths shared in the light of the bulb before sliding into the
darkness of the trap. I slid with less and less control in the
years that followed, knowing that the shared loneliness was
an illusion; that Miss Ewans had had company for some
time, not counting the presence of her sister. That illusion
was the trap through which I would slide in order to absolve
her memories that we somehow soon shared. Ashworth's
rustic could blend perfectly into the limestone of its native
and shrinking area of habitation, just like Miss Ewans when
she wanted to. I remember spying the limestone veins on
many of my walks, running my fingers along the chalky
white rock, partly in the hope of finding the moth on one
of the plants that grew naturally adjacent to it. The wings
of the Ashworth's rustic partly resemble a faded Rorschach
test, telling of some deep-seated trauma lodged within. I
remember sitting on a patch of grass bordered by limestone
rocks in the hope one would appear, though the moth,
however, never arrived; declining in numbers even then
due to many man-made environmental calamities. Despite
this failure to catch the moth, I enjoyed walking alone on
these Welsh paths and hills because they reminded me of
Miss Ewans.

I was not allowed to write or converse with her due to the great divide between her and my family, and could not have done so at any rate as there was no forwarding address for her new London house. The gulf between her and my family after Billie died never rejoined. It was only by chance that I would later find Miss Ewans again when in London, for my grandparents did not consider it worthwhile to even find out Miss Ewans' new London information. 'She is not worth a single word or thought of our time,' my grandmother would suggest, in the few moments when I foolishly showed my interest in Miss Ewans to still be present. She had failed to see, up to that point, that I was already mimicking the woman and following her down several paths, physically and mentally.

Walking one day through a forest in Snowdonia National Park, the exact part of which I cannot be precise on, a strange vision took hold, similar to that which occurred at Billie's funeral. The forest was framed with tall trees that seemed to never end in their ascent to the sky. The path was dark because of this but I caught sight of a copper blue and gave chase with some enthusiasm. Though a butterfly rather than a moth, and in this sense a complete waste of my time, I stepped after it off the path of the damp Welsh wood as flashes of blue darted between the tree trunks. The copper blue stopped in a clearing where the plants grew with more abundance, due to a greater density of light allowed in through a gap in the canopy. I entered the clearing too, but I felt my shoulders surge as the clearing gave way, dissolving before my eyes into what could only be described as a lake. The lake was not there and yet it was, though I could not move towards it. I could sense the gentle current of its water lapping upon the sides of a small jetty that housed numerous small boats. There was even a woman staring back towards me, sometimes turning to look out over the lake.

I did not call out to greet her or ask her what such a lake was doing in the middle of a forest. In fact, I could not move or speak at all and at once realised that, like the deathly flutter of moth wings that pervaded my mind at the funeral, I had become aware of my own detachment from reality. I could feel the spray of water from the breeze and sometimes felt a hand holding mine. I could hear black-headed gulls and knew that I was no longer in the forest chasing after the copper blue. This moment fades in my memory with each day, though I remember at the time almost instantly clicking out of this delusion and even forgetting about it for many years after, continuing to walk in the forest as if nothing unusual had happened at all.

After the death of Miss Ewans, I was searching through her photographs when I came upon a Polaroid. It showed a slightly descending green hill, littered with black-headed gulls. At the end of the hill there sat a lake, rippling in the breeze with a handful boats sitting on the water. I could not explain why a vision of this place had appeared before me in the forest whilst chasing the copper blue, but I knew that it would plague me if I did not at least try and figure out the whereabouts of this vision and what it meant. Miss Ewans had clearly taken the photograph. It conformed to her typical compositional eye for bisecting the photo with strong lines of land, water and sky. But, I questioned whilst sat in her living room holding the photograph, whose hand had held mine?

Several of these moments of synchronicity occurred in the dead time between losing contact with Miss Ewans as a young teenager and reconnecting in London several years later. I tried to fathom the cause of these moments, such was their accumulative, traumatic effect upon my own psyche. Often place would be emphasised, 'place being essentially the ghost of all our lives,' as Miss Ewans said one summer's day in her back garden. I imagined her amused look, peering over my shoulder when the synchronous moments occurred, and found much likeness between her past and my past, albeit my past already had hers intertwined within it. Such dizzying thoughts would plague my mind as if we were, in fact, the same person: a reflection of simulacra displaced by some impossible mistake. All of this could simply have been down to our shared geographies and our shared passions for walking and moths, but it went deeper than that.

I failed to shrug off the notion that our lives were somehow mimetic of one another. On another of my walking trips through North Wales, one of the very last before leaving home to continue my Lepidoptera studies in the capital, I found myself in a village somewhere in Snowdonia National Park, the name of which has slipped from my porous memory. At the centre of the village stood a church that seemed far older than the rest of the buildings. It predated the village. I had been attempting to catch several diurnal moths in the neighbouring fields whilst also mapping the area with my footfall, availing myself of some of the village's facilities, including a public house. I remember buying some food from its greasy counter, deliberately choosing something small and compact so I could eat it in the fields. But I did not go out directly into the fields, instead choosing to wander around the church and its graveyard, which I later ate in, sat on a mossy grave damp with plant life.

It was a luscious green stretch of land and the church seemed to sprout organically from the overgrown vegetation left with a benign neglect. I thought of the many different types of moths that would inevitably also avail themselves of this graveyard, sharing my taste for its quietude. I became so enamoured with the place that I took a photograph on a compact Polaroid camera that I insisted on keeping, despite the new range of digital cameras then becoming available. This camera was useless for photographing Lepidoptera, so I often wondered why I carried it around. It was a cumbersome camera but made up for such an awkward shape and size by taking reasonable pictures of landscapes, which I attempted to capture on almost all of my walking trips. I was never especially good at photography but took pleasure when such photographs came out well, or at least captured what I wanted from the landscape. The picture reflected the vegetation of the graveyard and church perfectly, though it rendered the sun on that day a brilliant white rather than the hazy emerald that hung in the air.

In the fields surrounding the village I caught several interesting specimens, which I stored instantly in the handful of jars carried in my backpack. They clinked together with each footstep, especially in this type of terrain. On one of my later visits to Miss Ewans, I told her of several photographs I had taken of this area, promising to bring them if she wished to see them. 'I would find that incredibly rewarding, Thomas,' she said. I felt that Miss Ewans enjoyed this elaborative game of show-and-tell. 'Do you recognise the place?' I asked, confronting her with the photo. She denied it almost vehemently, saying that she walked and caught moths further north, only passing through the area's more southern regions. I was unsure whether to believe her or not. Yet, when I detailed again the village's public house, she seemed to know the place well.

She very clearly shared my opinion of its questionable quality with an amusement which, to my mind, suggested that she must have visited it at some point, almost forgetting that she had denied ever having even been to that part of the region, never mind the village or its public house. It was only some years later, after her death, that this would be confirmed. It was on the same day that I found the single photograph of Billie, itself a pivotal moment in that it proved the existence of many hidden layers to Miss Ewans; even hidden from those whom she had trusted. One small box of photos seemed to consist almost solely of pictures and postcards from Miss Ewans' many travels around Snowdonia and North Wales more generally. I knew of her love for this area, and felt that I was knowingly following in her footsteps when I had walked there. It was only towards the end of a casual sort through these photos that I felt someone to have touched my shoulder. For, in a similar fashion to the lake that had appeared in the forest, I found yet another stark moment of synchronicity.

The photo that had caused this feeling was an old black and white picture of a church. It seemed a perfectly normal photograph: in portrait, bisected by the thick trunk of a tree. The spire of the church was hidden in part by foliage, and the parallel of the image, between the trunk and the spire, meant that the church looked as if it was grown rather than built. It was the same churchyard that I had taken refuge in to eat, away from the public house all those years ago. I stared at the photo, later taking it away to compare it with my own. It was indeed the same place, the tree on the left-hand side being the same tree that bisected the right of her photograph. Miss Ewans had visited this village, though she had insisted that she had not. She had even deliberately left evidence for me to discover that showed her word to be false; or so I thought.

I missed the mountainous Welsh regions once I was in London, but was glad to be finally living in a city, especially one filled with the excellent entomological departments that I needed for regular work. The air pollution, I believed, would also provide many interesting variations and evolutions of patterns of moth wings, first noticed by the Victorians many years ago. This would be the area of research that I would continue in after my initial studies as a bachelor of science, a point I would raise with my grandparents on the occasional visit back to Cheshire. 'Moving down to London had greatly enhanced my research,' I said to my grandmother on one visit. But I missed the Welsh hills that loomed over the minor Cheshire plains. Without these hills, I was alone.

Miss Ewans had not left a forwarding address when she moved, so when finally moving down to London from Cheshire myself, I barely considered the possibility of meeting her again. She could, for all I knew, have moved several times since, perhaps to the Continent, which she had often expressed a great appreciation for. But somehow, I knew that I would meet her again. 'Of course I will meet her,' I said to myself, sitting on a train down to view flats. I pretended to myself that I had forgotten all about the mysteries of Miss Ewans, but really I had done little else except follow her every move, miming the interests in walking and moths as if they were originally my own, when they were really hers. I was walking in Wales and catching moths there, just as she had done. I had even felt at times that I was Miss Ewans which, as a thought, would shake me to my very core. 'I am a boy and my name is Thomas,' I would often say to myself as a mantra, though it felt hollow.

It was mere months after I finished my degree and had moved straight into an entomology department near the Thames that I realised Miss Ewans was still in London. The department was north of the river, and I was engaged in a study of the cinnabar moth life cycle and the levels of population in relation to the spread of their food plant, ragwort. Preparing an admittedly dreary paper on the subject, I overheard one of my colleagues refer to Miss Ewans by name. The shock of seeing me become an animated and talkative person surprised my colleague, who had already grown used to my quietness. 'Is this Dr Ewans actually Phyllis Ewans?' I asked my colleague excitedly. He confirmed it and I found the new address through the reception, Miss Ewans often being engaged on a freelance basis for departmental research that required an expert on sphingidae: the hawk moth family. I remember the nervousness when I initially rang the number that the receptionist had provided, but my worry was unfounded, for Miss Ewans had already had a premonition of my call. 'If I were you,' she told me when I first visited her new house, 'I would have done the same thing.' The only constant when visiting Miss Ewans in those early days was reminiscing about Snowdonia, which I would partake in with relative gusto. We would relive with relish many visits to the area, and the highs and lows of attempting to find a variety of moths that only seemed to exist in the very lower parts of the hills and valleys. She seemed much, much older and I gathered that these memories were relived due to the increasing impossibility of her travelling so far. There was more to North Wales and its memories for Miss Ewans than she would say when alive though, but I found out much more after her death.

Among my most prized possessions is a pair of postcards that Miss Ewans wrote to her father when he was still alive. She made a point of never speaking about her parents, but she had written to her father on at least two separate occasions. She had stopped on the coast to post the cards, both of which depicted North Wales. It was very much on her way by car but, knowing her temperament and the strong desire she always had to mount and preserve her latest specimens as soon as was possible, evidence of her stopping in Colwyn Bay was especially poignant. The first postcard is dated in April, and shows the view out over the bay when the town was smaller but still clearly a popular resort. Miss Ewans writes briefly and generally in pencil to her father, ending the card with, 'Hope everything is alright, Love Phyl.' Perhaps, so I thought on finding the postcards, it was sent simply as evidence that she was still very much alive and well, something that parents need to know sometimes even when estranged from their offspring.

GENERAL VIEW. COLWYN BAY.

21471

POST CARD

FOR CORRESPONDENCE

FOR ADDRESS.

COLWYN BAY
2
20 APR

POSTAGE REVENUE 2D

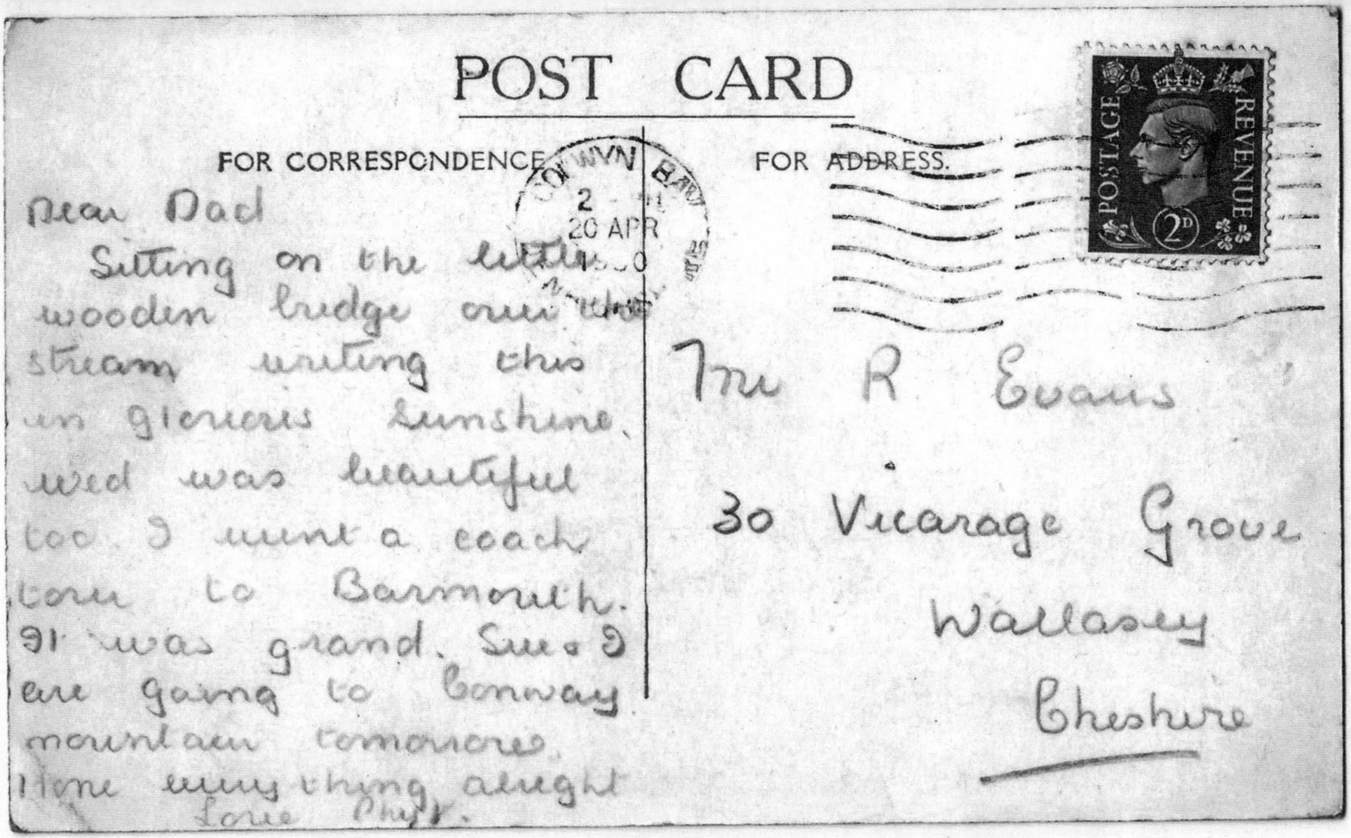

Dear Dad
Sitting on the little
wooden bridge over the
stream writing this
in glorious sunshine.
Wed was beautiful
too. I went a coach
tour to Barmouth.
It was grand. Sue & I
are going to Conway
mountain tomorrow.
Hope everything alright
Love Phyl.

Mr R Evans
30 Vicarage Grove
Wallasey
Cheshire

The second postcard was dated much later in the year, and hinted that this act of writing to her father was more out of necessity than for pleasure. Yet this one differed, perhaps in defiance, for the postcard in fact detailed Snowdon itself from the Caernarvon Road. 'This is my world,' Miss Ewans is saying through the image and, looking at them both after her death, I thought pleasantly of how we had shared this world. We occupied it at different times but we were both there, treading the seeds of our own mystery into the soil of the lower valleys. The postcard was simply concluded, 'My love, Phyl'. These Postcards were perhaps the only time I had proof that Miss Ewans actually used the word 'love' to anyone. Through them, I had a brief entry into her hidden life and the past which she had kept secret. It was this past that I desperately wanted to explore, where the secrets of the animosity between her and her sister resided, as well as where the other secrets of her life had been kept quietly and securely away from my questions.

SNOWDON FROM CAERNARVON ROAD

7050

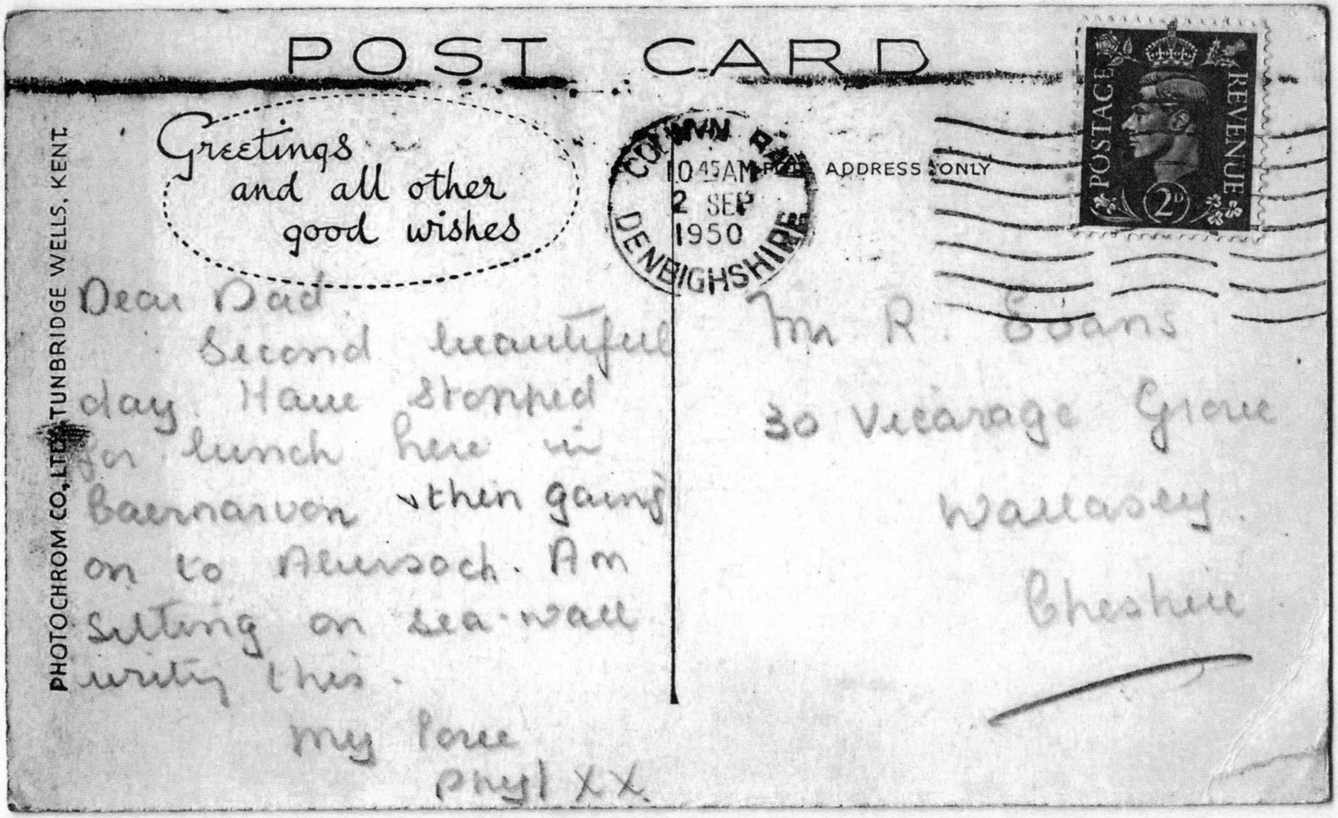

PHOTOCHROM CO., LTD., TUNBRIDGE WELLS, KENT.

POST CARD

Greetings
and all other
good wishes

Dear Dad
Second beautiful
day. Have stopped
for lunch here in
Beenavon then going
on to Alwood. Am
sitting on sea-wall
writing this.
my love
Cinyl XX

Mr R Evans
30 Vicarage Grove
Wallasey
Cheshire

ADDRESS ONLY

COLWYN BAY
DENBIGHSHIRE
10.45 AM
2 SEP
1950

POSTAGE
2d
REVENUE

My visits to Miss Ewans in London, which increased in frequency very quickly, were largely occupied with reliving her walking trips and the moths that marked them. Her garden there was much larger than her garden in Cheshire, and so she would regularly set her moth traps and sit in vigil over various lights and mechanisms, loading the large tub that made up the bulk of the trap with old egg boxes for the moths to stay dry in until morning. 'Once,' she said one evening whilst sat watching the moths fluttering around the light, 'I had somehow forgotten to collect the trap before it rained. It put me in a foul mood as I'd only just moved down here.' The vision of a small lake of rainwater filled with the floating remnants of drowned moths was described in detail. It would be a scenario ghosted many years later at a public moth-trapping event near the Thames that we both attended. 'The water,' she said, 'was light, as if oil had been poured into it.' She suggested, after initially struggling to remember further details, that she had poured the contents onto a flower bed and forgotten about it.

We would enjoy reading through her garden logbook detailing all of the catches that had occurred in her traps, some of which were killed and mounted on several displays hung on her walls. I enjoyed reading through this large book, its green leather binding becoming associated in my mind with a high standard of moth catching. But the book was also a temporal map of Miss Ewans' time in London, and so I felt that it somehow filled in the gaps between when I had lost touch with her and when I became reacquainted with her. The timeline of moths was a mere distraction, however, but an incredibly effective one. I took particular delight in noting the increase in copper underwing; an increase I knew to be directly due to Miss Ewans.

Like Miss Ewans, this moth taunted with its secrets hidden in plain sight, the beauty of its copper coloured underwing being teased out by its name. In reality, the wing to my eyes always looked more ochre. The moths were in her garden largely because of the proliferation of honeysuckle which she had bought specifically to attract a number of different species and their caterpillars that lived by the plant and its nectar. This plant was a sacrificial element in the garden, and was here uniquely to be eaten by a variety of different caterpillars and to produce enough nectar for several moths to proliferate. I noticed one day, whilst Miss Ewans was in her small kitchen preparing a tray of tea, that she had a small card that displayed an illustration of the plant alongside some wild rose. It sat under the prized poplar hawk moth, both items gathering dust.

The colour of the illustration, which presented an example far healthier and less caterpillar-ridden than Miss Ewans', seemed vibrant compared to the hawk moth above. The card was leaning against another frame that hovered on the wall just above the bureau. It detailed a loving note from someone whose name was withheld and who wished to organise a date to meet Miss Ewans. I was surprised, not just by the presence of something romantic, but that it was signed with such a loving phrase, 'Hope all is well with you so, for now, my fondest as always.' I quickly put the card back in its position leaning against the frame of the poplar hawk moth, and attempted to give the impression of having been sat idly waiting for Miss Ewans to bring in the tray of tea with the usual variety of stale biscuits. I diverted quickly, asking about a mounting of several different pug moths, which instantly and thankfully distracted from my worry over things that I could not understand. I only became more manic again when Miss Ewans mentioned that the motted pug was caught specifically because of the honeysuckle, again reminding me of the strange paradoxes that were building. She could see that I was perturbed by something and so – I remember this day well – she sat down and began to speak of an older time.

'It was in high summer,' she began, 'and the weather was perfect at dusk for a mass catch. I was in a field some way into the Midlands, though I can't remember where; you know how it is. For some reason, after a few hours of trapping, it became clear that there had been a proliferation of a variety of pug moths which seemed to be en masse in this patch of woodland.' She continued, suggesting that the number of pug moths became so great that it rendered further capture of them pointless. 'Every moth seemed to be a pug of some sort, all snuffling with their snout-like proboscises, failing to find the light,' she said with a laugh. She saw that her words had soothed me and I remember beginning to relax again. In return for stories such as this, I would tell of my own walks in search of a variety of diurnal moths. A field near the town of Llangollen provided the detail of one occasion, walking its pathways and attempting to chase many moths with my net, the jars jangling ominously in my sack as I recall.

Miss Ewans seemed curiously familiar with my stories, so much so that she would often attempt to hide her familiarity to them through an obviously false sense of surprise. 'A convolvulus, really?' she would say when I detailed a brief trip to the east coast on another visit. 'That must have been blown over from the Continent. I hope you had it mounted.' But it was a deception, for I knew that she was completely aware of the convolvulus I had found even before I had told her. Each detail was met with a nod of recognition as if merely confirming something of which she was already aware. 'You will have to show me the mounting you did at some point, I haven't seen a convolvulus for years,' she said. I never did show her the convolvulus, partly out of shame, for it was a tatty example very clearly blown over from the Continent on a strong breeze. But, more to the point, I felt that Miss Ewans had already seen the mounting. In my memory, she walks behind me on that trip, passing comment on various butterflies and moths. 'A holly blue,' cries a voice in my memory. It must have been my own voice, crying out when seeing the butterfly in the woods. But in my memory it is also Miss Ewans calling out after that flash of delphinium darting amongst the trees.

When such realisations occurred to me in her presence, I almost always left her house in haste. But when such realisations occurred alone, I would follow them through no matter how frustrating or stressful, in the hope that they would reveal their true meaning. My colleagues in the department would catch me daydreaming, sometimes shocked at the deep level of concentration I was in away from my work. 'Go for a walk,' they would often insist, especially after Miss Ewans had died; an event which they knew affected me greatly. This was when I was still at the department and before the great calamity of what could accurately be called my breakdown, in which the death of Miss Ewans cast my obsessions into a startling cage from which I could not escape. At this point, however, my drive to continue my research into diurnal Lepidoptera seemed to connect with my intrigue towards Miss Ewans and the stark coincidences that kept bringing us together. The studying of moths and the continuation of my research, so I thought, was equally an aid to knowing more about her. This relationship was cyclic. I failed to understand why this was so at the time, though I look back on it now with great fear and perhaps even resentment.

For a while I began to consider the likenesses between her logbooks and her murder mystery novels too, which became starker as the months passed by. Were these two differing collections of books not both concerned with the processing and collation of information about death? I only suggested this likeness once, for Miss Ewans was rather offended by the idea. 'Are your moth logbooks,' I began naively and light-heartedly one day, 'not in fact your own murder mystery novels? Do they not really concern your own killings and murders?' The sharp look she gave in that moment told me that I had progressed too soon in the comfort of knowing her once again. I recall trying to save the pleasant atmosphere that had been present only seconds before. 'But of course, it is not actually murder,' I said rather clumsily.

'They are alike in no way whatsoever, Thomas. How crass you have grown in our years apart,' she said. I knew that I was not to mention it again, but I continued, even years later, to secretly consider the likeness between the deaths in her novels and the catalogue of her killings in her moth logbooks. I would read them over and over after her death, considering how the variety of moths in her garden seemed to diminish in parallel to her body's ability to stay alive. The point in the books when her health finally failed, and when she required my almost constant attention and help, can be seen quite plainly. Her last capture, which I remember well, caught only a handful of common species and, with the setting up of the trap in the garden, there seemed no expectation of catching anything noteworthy at all.

There was a sense that capturing moths while clearly descending into illness was a mere gesture against the body or the separating of the body from the will, as I would later accept it to be. The trap was opened the following day and the small catch was slowly noted. The orange underwings and garden tigers flittered around, attracting several of the more confident birds from the neighbouring gardens, who had grown used to finding a veritable wealth of food scattered and disorientated. I wrote down the names of the moths, the number of each species, any interesting aspects of individual moths – the log of this catch recalls the frayed wings of a feathered thorn which must have hatched earlier than usual that year – and the details of the date and weather conditions of the evening of capture. This was like a murder mystery novel, I thought quietly to myself on the day of that catch, remembering the icy reception that Miss Ewans had given to the suggestion previously. She had slowly descended into the dazed phase that would become her normal state, and she didn't register much disappointment at the ordinariness of the catch. She failed to register very little at all, as I recall, but her presence was still felt; the enormity of her intelligence and character beginning to be set free from her body. My memories of the teenage years I had endured became markedly intermingled with memories that were not my own from this point, and I began to recognise someone else's memories becoming clearer. Miss Ewans' slow disintegration enhanced these feelings, as if she could transfer from her body to mine, almost conducting the melody of my déjà vu and memory of memories, so to speak.

The shock of first coming upon Miss Ewans and her link to my university department had felt both surprising and inevitable. I would maintain that such a connection was vital to both my own work and to potential breakthroughs for the department. 'I know for a fact,' I began one day in a casual conversation with a fellow researcher, 'that she has the most amazing moth collection, which I would wager has better examples of diurnal Lepidoptera than many of our own department's case specimens. They are,' I said with embarrassing overenthusiasm, 'almost a work of art. It would be a great coup for the department, perhaps even its saving grace in our current climate of funding cuts, to obtain and display such a collection.'

This was all conjecture in terms of the facts, for I had not properly become reacquainted with Miss Ewans when making such bold claims. But I could picture her collection clearly even before seeing it in its entirety after her death, viewing it through her eyes, her memories. I tried to use my interest in obtaining her collection to account for the feeling that I had become quietly used to: that there was something enormous missing from my understanding of the woman that I simply needed to know, in order to consider staying sane. I had become aware of this feeling even when first encountering Miss Ewans, though I was unable to properly cognise it: the feeling that there was something else in the room with us. It was also during this period that I first began to encounter the sound of moths outside of the normal occurrence at work.

I was used to the fluttering sound of the insect in the small numbers that I was able to capture in various traps. But the sound that had begun to reoccur, almost as a leitmotif for my mental anguish beginning with those early instances from my youth, did not correspond to the reality of the moths' fluttering as I had experienced it. The sound seemed to emanate from a horde, an impossibly large horde which would gather in volume out of sight, always behind the back of my head. The closest image I could connect to the sound was how I imagined the hordes of monarch butterflies to sound when gathering in large numbers. The butterfly migrates between California and Mexico in such great numbers that it renders the land a black and orange paradise, where every surface pulsates with wings. The sound they make must, so I thought, be similar to the sound that came to haunt my mind. Yet something was different about this sound. For I knew that it was created by moths. I am still not sure how I could tell, but the horde would haunt me more and more as my life began to revolve around Miss Ewans, tormenting with the cascading sound of their papery wings.

3

The more I spoke with Miss Ewans, the more our conversations became puzzling. There is little need to relate the extensive details of such conversations, as they were almost always framed around walking and moths but, with an unnerving regularity, I was plagued by a constant sense of déjà vu. This pervaded in both directions, by which I mean I recognised many of her memories of walks in the country and the capture of moths but, also, she greeted my memories with recognition too: as if we were one and the same through experience. This was not some kinship between people of similar backgrounds but a crossover that grew more alarming with each story, each moment becoming no longer my own.

Miss Ewans was to live for a number of years before I would acknowledge to myself that, in reality and in duty, I had become her official carer and I was not a mere confidant who spoke to her occasionally for pleasure. My visits multiplied with such speed that I seemed to be visiting her house on an almost daily basis, making sure she had food, fresh clothes, and that she herself was clean, just as my grandmother had done for her sister. In a house littered once again with dead insects and dust, this was an arduous and seemingly impossible task. Yet I took it upon myself to try my best and with no real request from Miss Ewans herself, merely a feeling that I had to. She needed to be healthy for as long as conceivably possible in order to pass on her secrets to me, so I thought. I would venture to her house after work at the university office, performing household duties whilst preparing to tell the many stories that I had eagerly prepared during my day.

This was an explicit requirement, as Miss Ewans seemed to draw energy from them, almost as nourishment. The quality of my work for the department decreased rapidly, or so my supervisor had suggested with a sad sense of frustration. I hated my supervisor, who was clearly someone who hadn't seen a live moth in years. He was the lepidopterist equivalent of a mortician, using others to do the work in finding and providing the cadavers, whilst he took the credit for the figures, the results and the publications. I told Miss Ewans about him regularly and the hatred we shared – mine through experience and hers through my experience – was a joy, and made the work just about tolerable.

I took to making slight alterations to previous stories when I eventually needed to concentrate on my research rather than her entertainments, changing details of the location or a moth slightly but using the genuine landscape in my mind's eye to add detail and truth. It became far easier because of this, requiring little time to concoct an evening's passing, finding everything that I needed in a matter of minutes. 'Of course, I caught a stunningly twig-like buff-tip on the east coast,' I would say. In fact, I caught several in various places, though never on the east coast. It was believable, and that was the main point.

Miss Ewans had really walked herself into an early grave, and it was obvious to both of us. Perhaps she even knew what she was doing and had bargained on having someone like me to look after her once her body began to decay. Her memory was slowly disintegrating too, and it was my job to keep it alight for as long as possible. This was relatively easy at first, as I seemed to access her memories simply by talking about my own. She would consider with recognition something long since passed that I had only just remembered, and I found this uncanny, though not fantastical. I first saw it as a sign of her pervading illness, her body and mind following the decay of the floating moth scales in the air all around. But I was mistaken, for she could add details missing from my own mind's eye with ease and which, when spoken, would miraculously make total sense and fit within the schemata of my inner world like a piece of a jigsaw puzzle. She completed my memories, even though it was abundantly clear that her own were collapsing.

On one occasion, I had stayed late in her house, it being a Friday and not needing to be in the department the following day. I sat at her side as the fire crackled, still relating stories to her even though I could see that she was gradually falling asleep, away from this world once more as the light faded. I remember the flames, now the only light illuminating the room, casting dancing shadows upon her face with a gusto that belied the tired canvas on which they performed. I was grateful for the fire, not only because it was cold, but because lighting it regularly would burn some of the debris in the air and make the main living room lose its stale odour, albeit briefly.

The room would, however, strangely refill the following day with more moth scales, of which there seemed to be an almost infinite reserve, as if they were derived from the mind. My voice was reduced to a whisper as I continued my story, this time about a reserve in the east of England that had recently been refurbished. I told of its excellent array of moths caught in their regular trapping session, and how I intended to visit it once more when the chance arose. I knew the chance would, however, only be possible after Miss Ewans had finally died, so I quietly meandered away from this point.

As I detailed more of the reserve's paths whilst sat on the floor of the front room, I felt a hand grasp my own. It was, I just knew, the same hand that had held mine in the forest in North Wales: a woman's hand, slender and friendly. I remember staring in the light of the fire, trying to break through the contradiction of my hand's emptiness here in the house. I had visited the reserve alone but knew that Miss Ewans had visited it several times too, and had even given a presentation to their society of moth enthusiasts – in more desperate times, as she had put it. She hated such events, which she would regularly bemoan as hobbyist rather than scientific. More unnerving than the feeling of the hand in mine was the uncanny change it seemed to make to my own. I looked down to my side in my memory of walking around the reserve and found my hand to be slender and feminine with longer, ill-kept nails.

My hands had never been especially masculine, my whole body in fact never really seeming either male or female apart from in the most basic of ways. But my hand was no longer my own, or at least the impression of my own. Miss Ewans was asleep when this occurred and I tried desperately to look further up from my hands in my memory. I traced the outline of the embrace of fingers as they hovered above the grassy ground of the path. The lower arm was that of a woman, and my arm was equally feminine. I followed the arm again and again, attempting to see the owner. 'I went to that reserve alone,' I told myself, but I was holding someone's hand there when recalling the day, someone who I seemed to hold a great deal of affection for. I could not look up to see who exactly it was, my perception dizzying and fading each time my eyeline reached just past the elbow. There was a feeling of nervousness about this. No one could be allowed to see us holding hands, whoever she was, I thought. It was not simply down to the fact that our affection was a secret, so I thought, but that it was considered highly improper as well. The image fell apart with every attempt to look up, denying a view of the other person's face again and again.

I squeezed my eyes tightly shut, as if to give power to the memory in order to explore it further. But it was to no avail, as the crackling fire kept returning me from my dreaming. I considered briefly who this person could be, and remembered the one brief romance I had had which, like most of my own social relations, had ended as soon as my obsessions with walking and moths had become readily apparent. My muttering about the hand woke Miss Ewans up from her slumber and I remember the appalling lies I told to try and explain this odd behaviour, even by my standards. 'You should probably get some rest,' she told me gently. But I was not ready to leave on this occasion and began to talk once again about the reserve, its proliferation of swallowtail butterflies and how it had a brilliant record of hawk moth sightings, despite their decline almost everywhere else around the country. It was a ruse on my part as I wanted really to discuss her visits to the same reserve.

'What was it like when you went, before it had been restored?' I asked her. She began to detail how shoddy the pathways were on her visit, but also how the natural overgrowth of many of the plants and reeds meant that there was a far greater variety of moths and caterpillars, surprising as the neighbouring farm had infamously ignored the restrictions on pesticide use, which had killed off a huge array of invertebrate life. 'We are living in the aftermath of the catastrophe of farming,' as Miss Ewans often put it. I shared her sadness about this but I had another point to pursue outside of the decline of insects. 'On your visit, Miss Ewans, who accompanied you?' I asked with surprising confidence. 'I was alone on those visits, Thomas. I always walked and caught moths alone, as you know.'

With her health deteriorating further, it was decided that I would help her to see some last sites and places rather than be cocooned in her living room. Perhaps, so I thought, I could show her some moths in the wild just one last time, though I knew it would be difficult to get her to a reserve in her debilitated state. The likeness between her decline and her sister's was quite astonishing, and it was only when visiting one day in the early spring that I noticed that she even wore the same blanket as Billie had done in the months before she died. It was an ominous discovery that added a sense of finality to the months ahead. She would not survive the year, and I began my mental preparations for the likelihood of her death. My visits were no longer those of a curious friend desiring the secrets of her past life, but those of a caring relative.

Behind the cobweb that increasingly obscured her view, however, I could sense a deep knowledge and awareness of both the present and the past which sometimes cut sharply through her general daze. The future, on the other hand, was an inevitability that both of us were acutely aware of and were facing together. The thought of life without Miss Ewans, or life without the truth of her mystery solved, was incomprehensible. I would have to deal with it later, in the hope that the ashes of disintegrating memory would allow such secrets to float out from their hidden place of their own accord. And so I began taking Miss Ewans out once a week to different places, largely country houses with their splendid gardens that required little walking. This latter point quietly depressed me: Miss Ewans could no longer be interested in both moths and walking.

I took to intensive research of buses and train routes to desired destinations, though we often resorted to special taxis that had space to house the wheelchair the local authority had arranged for her. I joined the National Trust in both of our names and made sure that the membership was well used, visiting endless regal properties and their vast array of gardens, traditional and botanical. I had ulterior motives for these visits, however, in that such gardens were a great draw for insects and so I could re-engage with my own passions for day-flying Lepidoptera. One Saturday I organised a trip for Miss Ewans and myself to the Elizabethan house of Penshurst Place in Kent. Though the house and garden were a draw in themselves for a lonely young man and a dying old woman, I had heard rumours that drew me there with an even greater pull. A colleague had suggested some time back that the property had a wall of various potent-smelling plants, on which a handful of hummingbird hawk moths regularly decided to avail themselves. I thought that such a sight would also be beneficial for Miss Ewans if we could find them, and the trip went smoothly. I remember her drinking in the sun as I pushed her around the garden, its rays pouring through the dust that hung in front of our eyes, interspersed by expensive scones and tea which neither of us really wanted.

Whilst walking in the gardens I was conversing for both of us, which seemed perfectly natural. The paths were incredibly rigid, typical of the Elizabethan fashion, requiring turns with the chair that were too sharp to make in one go. I was heading to the north side of the garden where the array of potent plants was supposed to be, and the spot highlighted itself with many flashes of colour darting above it. It made the house seem dead in comparison. The butterflies, bees and virtually every other conceivable insect were all involved in the pleasured frenzy of proximity to the plant. It was astonishing yet unsurprising, as the plant's odour even carried around the corners of the garden. I parked Miss Ewans next to it and the smell of its pollen gradually began to rouse her from her slumber. She was more awake than I had seen her for some months. 'This is a beautiful spot you've brought me to, Thomas,' she said quietly. The voice seemed disembodied, as all voices do when spoken by someone with their back to you, but also when someone's voice is considerably more powerful in spirit than their own body can convey.

It was her spectre that spoke more as her age took her under the waves, and I often felt as if I was walking side by side with her ghost whilst inconspicuously pushing her corpse along in front; her frail but edged words floating back into the air. I sometimes even addressed my replies to her infrequent statements to my left, where I envisioned her to be walking alongside me, rather than downwards to what more and more seemed like a cadaver. 'I'm glad we've come here,' she said, before taking her time in silence to try and observe the insects that were flying around the plants. Her head creaked from left to right, clearly identifying the insects one by one. I was surprised her eyesight could still make out the fast-moving invertebrates, though this may merely have been a gesture to acknowledge the effort I had gone to in taking her there.

The flash of the hummingbird hawk moth always produces a brief shock of excitement to the system. The insect, which is named for the obvious reason that it resembles a hummingbird in both its size and the way it hovers over plants while feeding, flittered past with that wonderful agility which gives the illusion of watching a stop-motion animation with several frames missing. The eye can avoid blinking for as long as it likes, but the hummingbird hawk moth still darts and defies our dimensions with ease. 'I have brought you here, Miss Ewans,' I whispered, 'because there are several hummingbird hawk moths.' I saw the realisation brought a pleasant reaction, for she tapped her fingers on the side of her chair with a sense of excitement. I caught sight of one of the moths again and quickly manoeuvred her chair to face the vast array of plants in order to see it. The moth stayed hovering around a small group of buds, which allowed her to see it at incredibly close proximity.

I briefly regretted not having brought my net or even a basic bottle, for it would have made an easy catch. The moth seemed to bring life to Miss Ewans, each dart of its movement providing her with that same jolt of excitement. Her head lifted and I remember seeing a physical change in her composure just from seeing such a beautiful moth. Miss Ewans had been stuck inside her house for six days a week and for so many months that each event like this, I believed, brought her an extra few days of life. I stood by as she sat watching the butterflies and the hummingbird hawk moth for a pleasant while. For one brief moment, I thought we had traded places and that I was in fact sitting, or wasn't really there as myself at all. I soon awoke from this state and made to pull her chair away from the plant, but Miss Ewans began to speak and so I stopped.

'I think I've been here before, Thomas, or at least near here,' she said. 'There's a village nearby where I stopped briefly on a trip back from the south-east coast once, don't ask me where. Did we come through a village? I imagine we did. We should try and stop there on the way back if possible, Thomas: the wood opposite it has an excellent variety of hawk moths.'

'Why was this village important to you, Miss Ewans?' I asked, but she merely drifted off the point, briefly mentioning a good number of feathered thorns caught in that village's forest – a personal favourite of hers, judging from the many mounts she had made of the moth with a variety of different colour variations.

The day was at a close, and so I took Miss Ewans back to London after a brief look around the house and the rest of the grounds. Though we made the most of such visits, I knew the houses were of little interest and more of a distraction. When we arrived back and I had arranged her into the corner spot in the living room once more, the fire was slowly lit even though the sun shone outside. She insisted that I bring her a box of photographs and some mounts of hers to look at. This took a great deal of time, at least with finding the mounts, because the ones she insisted on seeing were stored in her loft. The photos were in a cupboard with a large array of other boxes of photos, and were labelled 'English Adventures'. The loft was dusty and filled with mounted moths, old china and unusual piles of floral fabric. Her excellent and astute labelling meant that I found the plate that she was after relatively quickly, however, once in the loft itself.

Through the thick layer of dust, I could not see exactly
what the moths were in the framed plate, having identified it
only by the number which was stuck on the side of the frame
with a long paper label, aged to the point of almost blending
into the wood. Bringing all the required paraphernalia into
the room, Miss Ewans asked that I first go through the
photographs. 'You'll know what it is you are looking for
when you find it,' she said to me dreamily. I pulled out a
handful of photographs, and began to flick through them. I
had yet to see these, and began to become distracted by the
fragments of her life now open to me. She had never allowed
such access to this past before. Each photo yielded new
questions, new places that I now learned she had visited.

Then, with a shock, I noticed a small picture of a village.
I was shocked because, contrary to all the villages we had
been driven through to get to Penshurst Place, this one stood
out clearly as having been on our journey. It had not changed
even slightly, the white houses gleaming in the sun adjacent
to the forest where the feathered thorns were meant to thrive
in great numbers. The road in the photo was empty and I
imagined it just as the taxi had driven us through, not all
that far from the stately home. It was another ghost-step
that I had walked with Miss Ewans. I put the photograph
to one side, and remember taking advantage of Miss Ewans
falling into a quiet doze, using the time to consider the
meaning of the day's events. I picked up the dusty plate of
moths, briefly forgotten in my excitement at the photograph.
I wiped away the layer of dirt, half expecting to see feathered
thorns with their white antennae and triangular posture.

But the frame contained only two moths, both mounted beautifully. They were hummingbird hawk moths, set apart from each other and incredibly decayed. I thought of how these moths were ill-suited to being mounted, how their rapid speed was almost their entire draw. Then I caught sight of the writing underneath: 'Hummingbird hawk moth – Macroglossumstellatarum – caught near Penshurst Place, date unknown.' I recall looking up sharply from the mounting, ready to demand answers to the games Miss Ewans was clearly playing, the frame trembling in my hands. The fire crackled as its flames danced shadows once again on her face, for she was in a deep sleep, far away from the house.

After this trip, my memory of life blurs in that Miss Ewans declined at such a rapid rate that death seemed to be almost instantaneous. I was virtually living with her in these strange days, during which I felt as if some part of me was coming full circle. I became obsessed with thoughts of life after Miss Ewans or, more accurately, worried about how little I understood her still. My thoughts wandered to a future where the intense study of moths would somehow, optimistically, be enough to keep my stamina for life going, but it seemed improbable after knowing her. Yet, with Miss Ewans seeming to deliberately leave a trail of clues to follow, I also knew that I would not dive deeply into my studies again for some time. I would instead take to studying and solving her mysteries, her estrangement from her sister, the constant parallels between our lives, and the third person who seemed to stalk both of our memories. She was moved from her usual spot by the fireplace in the living room to a new cocoon upstairs in bed. She sat up in the bed, motionless, as I continued to try and bring life to her through my own recollections. She said very few words during this period, or at least I remember very little of the few she said. I find it difficult to recall any details because she really seemed more alive to me after her death.

The many dead moths were of great prescience to her during her few remaining moments of lucidity in these final days. I felt increasingly as if only I heard my stories of walking in search of moths, though I do recall some moments of acknowledgment. I had taken to bringing down more and more plates of the moths she had captured over the years, with specimens from Bilbao, the hills around Strasbourg and some private gardens on the Swiss–Italian border, among others. Her eyes flickered as I lifted each mount, first examining which moths were pinned to the boards and looking for any details written on the mounting paper of where they were captured.

'Do you remember where you caught these?' I would ask Miss Ewans, knowing full well that, even if she did, she would not have the energy to answer me. I would then begin to fill in the details of the trip, imagining the paths and walks that had led to such a capture. I found my own imagination to be far more active than I first perceived, seeming to grasp details with a surprising ease. 'These must be my memories too,' I once whispered to her, to which she gave a rare smile. The performances grew more and more tiresome as she faded away and I was in denial about her needing to be in the care of medical professionals. Eventually I gave in and organised her move to the hospital in which she was to die.

In the week before she was moved, the whole of her house seemed to be in temporal stasis. It felt difficult to move around within it. I began to tidy the messy rooms in between looking after her, arranging objects into neat piles, beginning to clean shelves and furniture, removing the layers of dead moth scales and empty chrysalises from caterpillars raised in jam jars but long since released. The house pre-empted my every move as if still under the control of Miss Ewans, even though I knew that she was upstairs in bed, virtually incapacitated with the illness of age. It seemed as if the house resisted my attempts to remove the natural chaos that had always dominated. But my movements of these objects seemed to disturb Miss Ewans too. Moving some of the old murder mystery novels, boxes of photographs and stacks of Lepidoptera paraphernalia awakened her for several brief moments before the men in the ambulance eventually came and took her away.

As I moved the many things, I thought that I would use them later as a map to find the heart of her secrets. She was leaving me the means with which to communicate with her after she had departed. It occurred to me that I had not really needed her alive at all, and that most of what I required was probably right here in the house. Miss Ewans was to prove me wrong, however. I began to contemplate what I was to do with all the objects that I didn't require, and became lost that week in daydreams about organising and tidying the many possessions around me. The chaos was a subtle defence against my questioning gaze, so I thought.

When the men eventually came for her, I had prepared a small suitcase of clothes, which even then I knew she would not need. I was surprised that she survived the brief trip to the hospital, which reminded me of the days when Billie was dying. There was no grandmother around to help organise the smaller details this time. Helping Miss Ewans meant helping myself, or so I thought as I finalised the packing of her things that night. She seemed to simultaneously know nothing and everything about what was happening. I caught a glimpse of her pale eyes, a last look at the dusty hallway and its walls covered in her beautiful moths. She was still trapped inside her body, but equally I was trapped in mine, frozen as I watched the woman forcibly removed from her house. I naturally accompanied her in the ambulance to the hospital and spent some time with her as she acclimatised to the antiseptic nature of the ward. I thought I had better distract her from the events unfolding and, once she was firmly settled into her new bed, I made a point of highlighting the small clump of trees outside of the ward's window. 'I bet there would some excellent catches if we were to set up a trap there,' I said. Miss Ewans didn't need my consoling; she had already drifted far away by that point.

'The moths will be fluttering by your window as soon as it's dark,' I said. 'They will be trying to get in, just to see the light.' Her sternness was gone, the characteristic which had defined her personality for so long. She sank finally into her bed sheets and faded into the air. The last thing she ever said to me aptly concerned moths, but it was really a further lead to continue my discovery of her secrets. She looked up in the afternoon before the evening that she died, and simply suggested that the poplar hawk moth, the single mounted moth that had first caught my attention all those years ago, was now mine. I found this to be an odd suggestion because, as we had agreed several months previously, everything that she owned was to be left to me after her death anyway. I would no longer need to live in my own small flat, as I would soon own her house. I knew, however, that I would never live in the house where Miss Ewans had lived. 'The poplar hawk moth is yours, Thomas,' she said, 'it is yours and it always has been yours.' These were the last words she would say to me, and I was glad that they were something we agreed upon. Later that evening she died and I felt, in those lilac moments that gently descend after a death, that she had not existed at all.

I had never organised a funeral before. After she had
died, I stopped referring to her as Miss Ewans, or even
Dr Ewans, and reverted to calling her simply Phyllis
Ewans again. This was because I needed to write her full
name many times on certificates, meaning that it became
a habit once again to refer to her by her full name. Now,
without being able to indulge in the obsession of learning
about her, sharing her memories and attempting to find
the source of why I found her such a mystery, I required
a new way to approach the subject. The first thing this
required was that I should no longer call her Miss Ewans.
It reminded me a little too much that she now shared
more in common with her sister and she had never really
cared for her academic title either. 'Bad memories there,'
as she had once said. As soon as the proceedings began
to officiate her death, the chaos caused by Phyllis Ewans'
absence during the arrangements for her sister's funeral
came starkly to mind. I had little help to fall back on, and
even my grandparents refused to come to my aid. London
was too far.

I had never been good at paperwork, especially that
which concerns people. It seemed abhorrent to me, yet
I felt it made little sense that I was not good at such
arrangements, considering my work and passions had
been explicitly about the arranging and filing of dead
things, albeit moths rather than people. I wished for a
long while during those weeks that Phyllis Ewans was
herself a moth rather than a person. I could have had
her mounted, stored and referred to her with ease, not
requiring meetings with solicitors organising death

certificates, funerals, burial, wills, money and everything else. The death of a moth is far simpler by comparison: into the killing jar, chemically arranged, mounted and catalogued, and that is if it's not simply released after a brief study, as is more common. I was sure she would have appreciated the comparison, though I suppressed a quiet resentment towards her as she had left little in the way of directions to follow after her death, other than my inheritance of her property.

I managed to get through the tedium of the paperwork by making sure that I intensified my personal study of her moths in between the meetings that I needed to attend. I would stay up into the early hours of the morning, working my way through her plates and mounts, determined to catalogue the collection fully at some time later in the year, endeavouring to then present it to the department of the university. This would, so I thought, make up for my shoddy work of recent months. 'Look at this splendid collection,' I pictured myself saying to the head of the department, taking pleasure in imagining the look upon his face as I presented the collection, perhaps at an event specifically ordained to herald the arrival of such a staggering display of Lepidoptera. First, however, I had to make sure Phyllis Ewans was safely in the ground, and that I was fully recovered from the mourning that I was already beginning to drown under.

I had never mourned before. Death had always been associated with the sisters due to Billie, whose passing was the only one I had any memory of. Reactions to death had always been either cold indifference or frustration on my part. I could not understand how Phyllis Ewans had been so cold about the death of her sister, however, or how my grandparents had managed to remain so focussed when organising everything. It seemed to require a total reduction of all feeling in order to do it properly. I considered why this was, as well as why so much paperwork was required. I concluded that it was deliberately to take advantage of those in mourning, paying as much as could be afforded to the required people, all of whom knew any price could be asked if it meant that the logistics would be sorted more quickly.

The solicitors and lawyers, so I thought, reminded me of certain forms of parasitic wasp who lay their eggs in the caterpillars of butterflies and moths. The young wasp hatches and eats the larva from the inside out, usually when they are in their cocoons metamorphosing. These men – for they were always men – reminded me of these wasps and I couldn't help but recall an occasion from my youth in Cheshire. On walking back along a path and field with my grandfather some years ago, we came across an extremely angry looking caterpillar of the puss moth. This caterpillar is a daunting and surprisingly aggressive larva, blessed with what looks like a bureaucrat's face and a lupine double tail, spending most of its life a shade of green before turning purple when ready to pupate. We took it back home and, learning that it built its cocoon from debris, supplied it with various twigs and wood, with which it constructed a suitable house to metamorphose within. For months afterwards I waited to see the moth emerge, famous for its size and design. Sometime later, we arrived home to find the wooden cocoon open, but in place of the expected moth sat a huge parasitic wasp. It was bigger than any I'd ever seen and streamlined black, flying around the jar in aggressive circles. We failed to identify it but it was just like these solicitors and bureaucrats, waiting for death to hatch within. I did my best to fend off these wasps, though I still fear that my own larva is waiting inside my diaphragm, ready to feed.

The funeral was organised for a cemetery in London, and Phyllis Ewans rested briefly in a private chapel which I chose not to visit. One of the few directions she left after her death was regarding the photographs to be used in any pamphlets or handouts for her funeral. The first she chose was a picture of her when she was much younger, a picture I remember her describing to me with a rare sense of pride. 'Don't you think I look like a scientist,' she had said to me one day, many years earlier. I concurred, and considered that I had not seen any photos of people that looked more scientific. This photo was to be on the header of the pamphlet though, in reality, only one other person would show up to the funeral to see it in spite of sending many invites to various colleagues and to a random assortment of people in an address book I had found.

The other photograph was of a vase of flowers, which was to be set at the end of the pamphlet according to her will and testament, after the words of a poem she had chosen to be read. I fail to remember the poem and, as there were only two other people at her burial – one being the priest – it wasn't even read out as the dirt was thrown on top of her coffin. I remember two very particular things from when I threw my clump of soil. The first is that I had brief lapses in perception again, and was momentarily plagued once more by the sounds of fluttering. Such a sound had an accumulative effect upon my visual perception, which once again seemed to see the wings of dead moths fall and float down into the grave like snow.

Unlike at Billie's funeral, however, I was stronger and resisted the motion of the wings. My body wanted to fall in on top of the coffin, as if I was also to be buried; that it was wrong that I was now separated from Phyllis Ewans and the paradox of us both existing had now broken. We were now different people. The second aspect of the funeral that I remember is the other person who attended. I was surprised that anyone had turned up at all, but then I began to wonder who this person was. It was a woman, not quite as old as Phyllis Ewans, but still a good deal older than myself. She wore black but I did not recognise her. Who was this standing at the graveside of Phyllis Ewans? I did not know and foolishly did not ask. It didn't seem to matter, especially after the moth wings floated down into the grave and covered the coffin. I somehow knew that I would find out who this person was, not because I had spoken to her, but because, underneath my lack of recognition, there was something I felt I knew about her.

Organising the objects that had accumulated over the years in the house was a task requiring an incredible amount of work and time. It became apparent that the initial paperwork was only a foreshadowing of the true work ahead. For Phyllis Ewans' house was arguably a map of her inner memory as much as it was a semi-detached property in London. Because of this, each object needed a great deal of attention before being logged, organised and sorted. Each piece had to be treated as potentially containing some clue about the mysteries of her life. Being obsessive in my need to sort and organise everything was also a great help. Sometime after the funeral I began this process of organisation, in spite of knowing what impact it would have upon my already decimated work rate for the university department. I had, by this point, stopped going in altogether after an incident that occurred a few days after the funeral. I had decided to head into the department office to ask for sick leave, or mourning leave. Initially it was my physical appearance that had alarmed my fellow researchers for, as only became clear to me then, my life with Phyllis Ewans had cocooned me from an awareness of my own dishevelment. The shock was all too clear on the face of one colleague, who asked with a worried tone if I was all right.

The incident was not, however, simply the noticing of my haggard appearance, but concerned meeting another colleague a few moments later. I needed some paperwork about the status of my current flat, keeping all such necessary paperwork in the office. All things that I considered to be work – all things that were not part of my interests in moths, walking and Phyllis Ewans – were kept at a distance. But my visit was to be chaotic and cause much concern among my colleagues, as my visions of fluttering wings began to plague me once more as I walked through the corridors.

The fluttering grew worse and I recall feeling incredibly faint, so much so that I had to crouch down on the floor to avoid the cacophony. 'Who let these moths escape?' I supposedly shouted at great volume. Though I was later told that it was a fellow researcher from my department who found me, I can only recall being met in the hallway by Phyllis Evans – as she was when I had known her as a child, now able to walk once more and grimacing out of character at my pathetic position. 'Where is Phyllis Evans?' I supposedly asked another colleague. I began to consider this a grand scheme, using my mourning and exhaustion as a ploy to get rid of me from the department. I could see through their ploy, their desired destruction of all my work, and ranted at them about how they were going to lose the best collection of moths that I, a researcher in Lepidoptera, had ever come across. Even if they believed me regarding the collection, so I thought, believing or disbelieving could be part of their ploy to oust me too.

I was not to return there, even after I had concluded my investigations into the mysteries of Phyllis Evans, though at this point I was given several weeks' leave to recuperate. I was still suspicious of such an action but accepted and considered it a great advantage. It gave me a deadline to sort out the possessions, and I knew that I always worked better to deadlines. I left the department and collected some clothes from my flat. I was to move into Phyllis Evans' house, determining to sort and organise everything, setting up camp in her bedroom. The room was the barest in the whole house: that is why I chose it. In other words, it required the least sorting and tidying, but it meant that my mental state began to slide further than I could ever have conceived. My thoughts would regularly become lost and no longer my own. I found myself in long daydreams, staring at the wallpaper with its singular two-stripe pattern. My eyes could not see the present, only what I deemed to be the past. The past was now my garden, littered with dying plants eaten by caterpillars, which had left them grey and rotten. The bedroom was the worst room I could have chosen to sort first: it was the most potent with memories of Phyllis Ewans that I had yet to experience. The memories of this room became mine, the quilted duvet was mine, the rug was mine. I indulged in this lapse of reality by bringing in small boxes of photographs from the cupboard downstairs to aid the delusion.

Rifling through them, I could see that organising the house was going to take a great deal of time, especially as the movement of my whole body had become slower since seeing Phyllis Ewans in the corridor of my university department. My limbs felt heavier after the vision, as if I was the one who was now older than Phyllis Ewans. Our relationship had always been defined by my youthful energy being of use to her, to draw from when her own body began to weaken and fade. Now, even though she was dead, she felt younger than me. We had seemingly switched places. I assured myself that organising and sorting the house would readjust this feeling. It would confirm that she was dead, for she was not dead to me at this point but very much alive. She was becoming me, or perhaps I was becoming her; it mattered very little which way round it was. Contrary to what I had believed would happen after her death, I did not feel surer about the difference between us as people. Instead, I felt that the line had been further blurred.

I decided to take a picture of the room, which was now tidied so that I could sleep in it comfortably. It was taken on an old Polaroid camera of Phyllis Ewans' rather than my own, which had a handful of photos still left in it. I held the Polaroid photo in my hand, staring at it and comparing it to how the room looked through my eyes. It was still her room, no matter how hard I tried. I brought in several plates of moths, some faded garden tigers in various sizes and types, their bright orange elements no longer providing the wonderful contrast to their defined black and white forewings. I had lost this room even though I had worked hard to make it my own, to make a base away from her influence. To understand the shared nature of our lives, this house needed to be taken apart, organised and catalogued. As I lay on the duvet that night, I thought to myself about the kudos I would receive when presenting the collection of moths to the department. I will present her moths to my department, I thought, and I will know Phyllis Ewans and not become her. I had a great deal of work ahead, I thought, falling into a brief sleep; plagued by dreams of a woman's face peering with hollowed eyes from the corner of the room, through a mist of dead wings.

4

My need to dominate Phyllis Ewans' house grew to startling proportions. In my mind, I was convinced that the quickest way to answer my questions regarding her life was to organise the house. Her life was, so I kept repeating to myself, now contained only within these walls, within these objects, these photographs, these dead insects, these unfinished papers on the breeding patterns of privet hawk moths. As my obsession grew, my appetite lessened; I allowed for the occasional daydream, which often involved the proud display of the new collection of specimens on the walls of the department: my crowning achievement for an underfunded and disavowed segment of the university. My daydreams would continue, shaking hands with people more important than I was, showered with gratitude for the immense amount of work it clearly must have taken to organise, document and restore the many moths in the collection.

Before I could earnestly sort out the moths and give them the attention they deserved, I had to organise the other dead

things in the house: namely, the memories of Phyllis Ewans. I
knew this would take a great deal of time, for as soon as I had
begun, the mental difficulty which the objects created for me
rose up with a regular intensity. Soon I moved to the main
areas of interest: the office room upstairs, the living room
and the spare 'junk' room downstairs. I wondered whether I
would encounter any memories of earlier years, of Billie and
the time my grandparents became part of Phyllis Ewans' life.
It would have been a pleasure to revisit those times.

I was wrong, though, for Phyllis Ewans had removed
almost all traces of her time with these people, with the
exception of one photograph of her sister that, as already
mentioned, was used for the funeral pamphlet. I considered
that this was actually kept morbidly as evidence that her
sister was most definitely dead. I began to rummage deeper
into boxes and cupboards, disturbing thick layers of dust
and sending it into the air, every movement creating a dusty
spectre that followed my progress around the rooms. My plan
evolved so that, after finishing the barren office space upstairs,
I would begin the process of moving all of the moths and
moth-trapping memoranda into this room, telling myself that
this was the very beginning of the organising of the collection
for the department. This was to be the moth room.

The moths were the most difficult things to move, as they
seemed to hold the most power over my eyes, the hallway
and rooms regularly dissolving around me into country paths
or fields. Even more unnerving was the frequent feeling of a
woman's hand holding my own in an affectionate embrace.
I would be sitting in an intense moment of study, holding

an object in one hand, when I would notice that my right hand was lying dormant and cupped, leaning against my leg as if held there by another. This was not the spirit of Phyllis Ewans, I told myself, as she was left-handed and, if it were her, it would make little sense. She was very particular about not adjusting any movements to compensate for dealing with right-handed people, especially men, who she would make a point of forcing to shake with their weaker hand. It reflected her general mistrust of men, whom she considered generally idiotic. 'They cannot really capture moths with any great skill because it is a delicate violence,' she had once said. But I felt very strongly, when considering the spirit hand that held my own, that this was still the hand of a woman.

I would catch my thumb making a rubbing movement against the air, as if affectionate towards whatever it was that lay there. Or, more precisely, who it was that lay there. It was not that I could sense it was a woman who was holding my hand, but in fact that I knew it was a woman holding my hand. I seemed to know this woman and, when looking intensely at whatever object I was holding, I felt great waves of kinship washing over me, sometimes even distracting me from what I was attempting to observe. This would have been where she would have haunted if ghosts did exist, and if she existed as a ghost or spirit and needed somewhere to haunt. The hand that I felt unnerved me, however, and I observed that the grip grew tighter when my right hand held particular objects, as if the memories grew stronger through them. I noticed this especially when I came across an odd piece of card with instructions written upon it.

REGULATING A CLOCK.

IN THE CASE OF A
PENDULUM CLOCK, THE
PENDULUM BOB IS USUALLY
HELD IN ITS PLACE ON THE
PENDULUM ROD BY A NUT
UNDERNEATH THE BOB
TO MAKE THE CLOCK RUN
FASTER, THE NUT IS SCREWED
UP A LITTLE HIGHER SO THAT
THE BOB IS A LITTLE HIGHER
ON THE ROD.
(SLOWER - REVERSE)

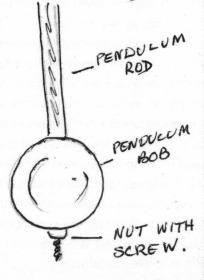

PENDULUM
ROD

PENDULUM
BOB

NUT WITH
SCREW.

On the card were instructions for regulating the pendulum of an old clock, and it detailed how to modulate the speed with which it swung. My hand felt the grip of the woman and it drew my attention to the object, which I was about to pass off as another piece of rubbish. I had not considered the card, or given it much thought, when it had tipped out onto the floor along with the other bits and pieces amassed in an old wooden drawer. The card had a small drawing of the pendulum and, as I felt the grip suggesting some importance unknown, it occurred to me that I had never seen any sort of clock in the house. After reading the card briefly, which seemed obvious in its directions, I put it down on the pile of receipts, photos and books, and began to look around the house for the clock. It was the sort of large object that I imagined was easily taken for granted, especially in the dazed state that I perpetually found myself in during that period.

After searching the entire house, including the loft, I could find no trace of any sort of pendulum-swinging clock. I wondered whether I had been imagining things, whether I had been too long in the house; a place where I was already hallucinating heavily after mere hours within its walls. My mind, I decided, was playing tricks upon itself, and so I made a point of handling objects and things with both hands, not allowing for one to hold the spirit hand. An image came to mind of standing in front of the clock, admiring it and feeling a woman's hands warmly hold my waist from behind. I was no longer in the room, but I fought quickly against this feeling. 'We were not meant to be so public,' I said skittishly to myself, before remembering that I was fighting a vision. I was alone in the room.

Soon after, I made a start on the many books that Phyllis
Ewans had collected. I had never seen her reading a single
one, but she had always looked bookish. If there was ever
someone who looked like they owned and read a great deal
of books, even murder mysteries, it was Phyllis Ewans. I
began to examine each of them, starting from the middle of
the shelf at random and working my way from left to right,
before moving on to each shelf below. Every book was old
and yellowing, the dust layer on top being a thick, grey
carpet that crumbled down gently when disturbed.

I had little interest in the books themselves, but considered
the possibility of them containing more than just the stories of
country house murders that the covers suggested. I would
observe the cover of each volume before placing the book in a
bag, soon to be taken to the charity shop further up the road. In
taking the books away from the house, the essence of the rooms
became simplified and easier to consider. Paying special attention
to one book, I stood up and flicked through its pages. It was the
volume that had the giant wasp on its cover bothering a small
plane, the volume that had attracted me when younger, before
the poplar hawk moth had taken hold of my attention. I briefly
considered keeping it, being the only other link I could find with
the Cheshire house aside from the hawk moth. It reminded me of
my awe at first meeting Phyllis Ewans, an awe which hindsight
seemed to portray as a meeting of old acquaintances rather than
the awkward first meeting that it actually was.

I looked up from the book and towards my own
reflection in the mirror. I stared back, at first not recognising

the person reflected back at me. I was visibly dirty, the dust from all the objects making my hands look particularly in need of a wash. I could barely make myself out, for I was not feeling myself at all. I knew that moving into the house would complicate my relationship with Phyllis Ewans, even if she was now dead and buried under mounds of scales. The finality of her death should have made it easier to forget that I secretly harboured the notion that I was her, but it made it worse. I was a mixed personality that was lost regarding which side to fall upon, which side to become.

Looking down, I noticed a ripped photograph on the floor. The object had fallen out of the last novel I had looked through. I bent down and the sharp, almost electric feeling that emanated from simply holding the photograph made my fingers briefly reflex in shock. It felt different to all the other photographs I had so far encountered because of its clearly secret status, and I felt the need to sit down sharply, as if the physical weight of it was too much for my body to take, weighing my arm down to the ground.

It was part of a brightly coloured picture, full of the greens and blues of memories passed from a faded sunny day. There was a wall and some greenery, clearly part of a garden, and a white house and roof made smaller because of a large, dark green hedge, no doubt obscuring the rest of a much larger house. The photo was bordered by a white line, and so it can't have been too old, judging from the nature of these chemist developing formats. I remember sitting for a long while under the strain of the implications of the photo. Had I been too blasé in throwing the other books away so quickly into a bag destined for the charity shop? I had unnerving thoughts of some future customer of the shop, one with a penchant for murder mystery novels and not in the least bit interested in walking and moths, opening one of the books only to find a photograph contained within its pages.

Even worse, the photograph would have meant absolutely nothing to them, whereas for me it would have meant everything. Finding this fragment of a photograph presented a memory that had been locked away, but one that was meant to be found. I wagered that she knew that I would come into possession of all of her books, that I would end up organising them and sorting through them, allowing me to find the fragment eventually. But what this fragment told me more than anything else was that it was only the first. I put it on the mantelpiece above the fireplace very carefully and noticed how there seemed to be a faint breeze, gently ruffling the objects that lay all around. The place had entered the room.

I checked the bag in which I had stored the other books for any more loose photographs, but none seemed to have fallen out. Repeating the action of days before, I then began to remove each book more carefully, flicking through each page with precision in the hope that more fragments would present themselves. The first shelf was cleared as the breeze in the room grew. I was roughly halfway through the second shelf when another photograph fell from a book. I fail to remember what the title of the book was, or what any of the titles of the books on this shelf were, due to the sheer excitement and manic behaviour with which I completed the task. The photograph was just as vibrant as the fragment, suggesting that the pictures had been taken in the same period. It was an incredibly blue picture showing a small harbour, undoubtedly constructed for pleasure boating rather than business, by some lakeside that I guessed was probably in Wales, the same place I had seen in an earlier photo and in my teenage vision in the forest. I could hear the gulls again, feeling the occasional spray of water on my face, becoming momentarily held within the photograph as if it was my own or, more accurately, as if I was at that moment in the act of taking it.

Most important was the presence of a woman on the quay, some way further back. In fact, the photo was really of her, and the delusion of the place entering the room was a mere distraction from her presence. She wore a white coat and very clearly was not Phyllis Ewans or anyone else I had seen in her pictures. I accepted the likelihood that Phyllis Ewans had taken the photograph of this woman, the framing having her touch of middle ground composition. I could see that there was a faint smile emanating from the woman, but it took a good while under a lamp to observe this detail. The curtains were drawn with the sunlight illuminating the room only through the colour and patterns woven into the fabric. I felt a sense of shame at the madness I was now allowing myself to live within. I had spoken to Phyllis Ewans about her acquaintances – never friends, always acquaintances – and she had never mentioned anyone who could fit the description of this woman. Even I was technically an acquaintance, and I had looked after her until death. I put this photograph with its air of mystery next to the fragment on the mantelpiece, staring at the pair together: the fragment and the woman.

Why had Phyllis Ewans gone to such a place with this woman? I felt briefly envious, before my envy dissolved into something far stranger: the feeling that I had no reason to be envious at all, as if I had been jealous of something I had done myself without quite knowing when. It seemed nonsensical, not because she was dead, but because I was alive and these were my thoughts. Our stories were one, though I was only halfway to gaining mine back. My youth was not wasted, it was twice lived. I continued my plunder of the shelf, sifting through each book in search of more photographs, more memories to be reunited with. 'I want to be reunited with you,' I said out loud. I had taken to speaking to myself a great deal in the weeks after Phyllis Ewans died. This was a logical turn of events, I thought, perhaps even sharing such an admission out loud as I had lost the ability to recognise when I was speaking out loud and when I was speaking within. I was now speaking for both of us, though I did not hear my own voice, with the exception of a few rare moments of realisation.

On the third shelf yet another photograph drifted out of a book. It began to make some sense and, with their being four shelves of books on this stack, I guessed there was one more to find. This photograph was darker than the previous two but was more important, for it portrayed the woman again but in greater detail.

The detail of her face came as a surprise, as I didn't expect Phyllis Ewans to have given so much away. The woman is wearing the same coat as in the previous picture but the light makes it seem far more yellow than it did by the lake. Perhaps the weather turned, explaining the darker look of the photograph. She is standing outside a bed and breakfast, a carpet of ivy hiding the stonework of the old building behind, giving the impression that it is now part of the architecture. This was a holiday, a feeling of reunion emanating from each photograph and from the thoughts that each photograph lit within my own memories. We had shared silences because we knew something indefinable. I thought of the woman who had been at Phyllis Ewans' graveside; but it was not her.

I began to consider this woman's hands in the photo. They looked like the hands that I had seen in my own on various occasions, the realisation of which felt like an unfounded yet natural assumption. I knew this woman from somewhere. She held a great affection for me, and even a sway over my thoughts. The photograph was put alongside the others on the fireplace and a picture was gradually building of a moment in time, perhaps merely a holiday to a regular viewer.

'It is more than that,' I said to myself confidently, uncaring about the pointlessness of such speech, unheard in the haunted house. My task was coming to an end and the findings had left me exhausted, a spirit left to float in a lonely room. I remember feeling distracted by the breeze that had grown stronger and stronger as more and more books had come off the shelves. There were no windows open, and I even made a point of checking that the room was sealed. The windows were closed shut with dirt and grime, rendering the curtains a needless enterprise. My movements disturbed great layers of cobwebs built-up on the fabric.

I began to take the books off the final shelf, growing impatient as each one revealed nothing, filling more and more bags, flicking through each book until all that was left on the shelf was a stray map of North Wales. It was clearly battered from rainy days out in the field. Its edges were torn and several of the contour lines had sprouted three dimensions from being left to dry whilst damp and crumpled. It took a great deal of time to open, because the edges were revealed to be increasingly tattered in each fold, telling of more stories than the words of the books ever could. The map brought back a feeling of pleasure that I could not let go of and I vowed that, on completing my tasks of organisation, I would rekindle such pleasure – my pleasure of maps, so to speak. Eventually, unfolding the part of the map of a specific region of Snowdonia, the final hidden photograph fell to the floor.

I joined it to the fragment that had fallen out of the first novel and stared at the reassembled picture. The small house in the first photo was not small at all, but an extension upon a much larger property. It seemed vast, with a huge garden that I recognised both from earlier photos taken out of context and from other visions. The house had been imprinted on my mind for some time, an anticipator of some future meeting that was always to happen. I concluded that this was the end of the trail, but I also knew that the woman in the photographs owned this house. She had lived there for many years and it had been a home of sorts. It was more than intuition; it was knowledge. This was a trail that needed to be followed in full whilst it was still warm, before I became trapped in a haunted past that was not my own. The idea was lost but the memory was there, waiting. I was now on my way to understanding Phyllis Ewans and I thanked her.

Upon the discovery of these photographs, my mind began to relax and became less frantic in its nature, providing a brief antidote to the mania. Though the lapses from reality grew worse, I welcomed them with an open and free demeanour, more than I had done previously. I was now properly on the trail, a genuine trail. Having paranoia confirmed as legitimate fact can cure most ill feelings developing in the mind. I took to my duties of organising the house with a surprising enthusiasm in the following days that belied my battered body and mind. The rooms became clearer as the days went on, arranging where things went and which things were to stay. The waste of time that I knew this to be provided great comfort. I had not taken any enjoyment from needless activities in a very long time. I knew that this was soon to be my house, or at least accepted deep down that it had always been my house in some sense.

I made the most of my journeys to the charity shop with the vast array of novels, now deemed unnecessary. They had outlived their purpose. It signified that I was making progress, but it also provided the chance to walk again. The walks to deposit the books had a cathartic quality as I took in more and more details of my surroundings, eyeing up neighbouring gardens and the beautifully painted doors of houses nearby. I built up a gradual rapport with the roads around as I repeated the journey, noticing the exact route each time. The woman in the charity shop came to recognise me as a sign of the impending arrival of murder mystery novels, and I noticed with each visit that very few of the books from my previous visits were there on my return, feeling a slight regret at their probable value and my lack of foresight in not attempting to sell them.

Even so, I remember saying to myself, as I was leaving the charity shop after my fifth delivery, that I would not be parting with a single one of the volumes on Lepidoptera. There were many excellent editions that I had yet to look through: editions that had illustrated plates as opposed to photographed plates. Perhaps the department would be grateful to receive them too, alongside the specimens that I planned to gift them. I knew that I would have to examine the volumes carefully and check for potential research projects, perhaps looking into some of the earlier lepidopterists and artists, before handing them over. I had always preferred illustrated plates to photographed plates, the detail being far more accurate, especially in regards to how the moths moved and flew in the night air. Once dead, the moths slowly lost their colour and the forced positioning of their wings into a fully open, pinned formation was as far from their natural behaviour as could be. Any moth alive deluded enough to be as confident in its posture as their mounted compatriots would soon find themselves equally as dead.

Sometimes I would see a younger Phyllis Ewans walking down the street towards me, passing me by as the pavements faded and ebbed between then and now. I took great pleasure in enjoying the memories of the times I had shared with her. I recalled one day when we had visited a reserve in London, perhaps the most well-known reserve in the city, though its name now escapes me. Phyllis Ewans had suggested we pay a fleeting visit because of a regular moth-trapping event that was held there on a weekly basis. She had not wanted to go to the actual trapping event, however. 'The amateurish methods they no doubt use would ruin my day,' she said. Instead, we endeavoured to visit the following morning to see what was caught, in the hope that the lack of experience would be difficult to perceive when distracted by the moths themselves.

Phyllis Ewans was still spritely for her years at that point, well before the illness of age ravaged her body and rendered her an invalid. I have fond memories of travelling with her on a train and then on the tube and bus, all of which she detested, giving a running commentary loudly for her fellow passengers about how much she detested such transport. 'This seat is filthy,' I remember her saying, 'and more to the point, so are the windows.' Waiting for the bus near Hammersmith was the worst part for her, and she vowed to head to the reserve from the south side of the river on future visits. Phyllis Ewans seemed visibly shaken by the number of people around even at that early time in the day. The reserve, when we eventually arrived, was quiet in comparison, very much because it was early on a weekday rather than a weekend, and the moths had attracted only a small group of local enthusiasts. Her arms were folded with impatience, tapping her fingers from her left hand onto her lower right arm with stark repetition. She had never possessed a great deal of patience, and was visibly annoyed at the organiser, who insisted upon waiting in case anyone turned up late to see what they had caught.

Eventually, the organiser began the process of opening the trap to see the catch, which was not a great deal. I remember this occasion incredibly well, at least in terms of what happened, for the scene was lent a surprising drama when it was discovered that, like the night some years previous in Phyllis Ewans' garden, water had entered the main barrel of the trap, caused supposedly by a rain shower sometime in the night. As the moths had slid down the funnel in an attempt to reach the glowing light of the bulb, they had slid down into a watery grave. The egg boxes that had been carefully arranged as overnight housing for the insects lay in a sodden mush, surrounded by oily-looking water from the scales and dead wings. A few were still alive, attempting but failing to fly due to being soaked by the water. 'I can't understand it,' the organiser had said with dismay, 'there was no rain last night and the top was covered. 'It seemed as though someone had deliberately poured water into the trap, though it was never confirmed either way. Some effort was made – with the help of Phyllis Ewans, who had more experience with such things – to dry some of the moths, and it worked for a few. The less damaged moths soon began to warm up in the London sun, coming back to life and wandering away slowly into the nearby grass. Others were beyond help and were thrown into the bushes for the birds, though their surviving counterparts didn't fare much better as a number of goldfinches came down to pick off the living. Phyllis Ewans didn't seem too disappointed with this result as I remember, and she seemed to relish taking charge of the proceedings ahead of the inexperienced young man running the trapping. The other participants could not hide their disappointment, however, clearly feeling that their interest and passion had manifested in a mass drowning of the things that they had so desired to see.

We then wandered around the reserve for a brief time afterwards to make the most of the day. Planes were flying overhead but the wildlife was entirely used to the sound and sight of such aircraft. The moth trapping had been an unmitigated failure, but we had had an enjoyable day. On the way back, in between complaining loudly about the abject state of public transport, Phyllis Ewans said something unusual. It was the reason why this trip stands out. After being frustrated at having to ask a young man to move out of the seats designated for the elderly on the tube, she started to discuss her relationship with death. 'I seem to need death for my work,' she said loudly. Such a statement caught the attention of several commuters and I felt embarrassed, but she went on, unconcerned by what the many suited men on the District Line thought of her need for death. 'We both need death in a sense, as it highlights our memories,' she said as the tube sped towards Victoria. Death was needed for our work in a practical sense because we both studied dead moths, but also in a general sense, in that we were working almost entirely to slow down the perception of the journey towards our end. The idea was prescient as, soon after this, Phyllis Ewans fell over onto a particularly hard floor in her house whilst moving an optimistic number of mounting plates.

The fall hurt her a great deal and, though despising the very idea of any sort of hospital, she was forced to go and have herself looked over. She had fractured her hip in the fall, as well as bruising her left leg badly. I see this as the moment that finally allowed her age to seep into her rebellious spirit. When age finds such a gap, the mind soon follows. Sometimes this can be vice versa if someone is unlucky but, for Phyllis Ewans, it was her body that was going to give way first. I have never seen a flooded moth trap since that week but I know that, if I was to unfortunately come across one, organised by some inexperienced moth-trapper, it would remind me of the moment when Phyllis

Ewans became old. This was the moment when she finally showed her age, and her body signalled to her mind that the two were not going to be of help to each other for much longer. I would look after her from this point onwards, her needs gradually becoming greater and greater until she eventually died in the hospital.

Walking back along the road to her house, ready to pick up yet another pile of novels to take to the charity shop, I passed her young self again, walking back the other way with a jaunt in her step. The pleasure I took from this vision was immense, drenched in the acceptance of her death but knowing that she would defy age and return again and again for as long as I could see her. The moths were arranged now that I was properly organised with my tasks in the house, and I made great efforts to clean and prepare them for what I imagined to be a great ceremony. I had yet to consider where exactly they would be stored or what specific use they would fulfil, but I was sure that there were specimens here that were in better condition than some of the department's older stock.

I also considered a paper dedicated to the contrast in periods of time and the differing effects that pollution had had upon the colouration, and perhaps even migration, of certain families of moths. It would be entirely viable as a project, I thought, due to how well many of the moths had been preserved, and how well-documented their place and date of capture was in the logbooks. It could have been a worthwhile research venture considering the alarming figures surrounding the decline of so many species, as if extinction was quietly taking place but on such a large scale that the study of it was virtually impossible. The plates were stacked up in the moth room and took up a great deal of space. There was no question of throwing any of them away: they may have been the very last of certain families of moths.

I sometimes thought that I could hear these moths in their casings, attempting to flutter their wings whilst still impaled to the boards by their pins. I would lie awake at night in bed, considering the sound. It felt as if I had granted some sense of freedom to them, but not freedom in a technical sense. Simply the movement from the darkened attic seemed to have constituted some freedom. Such a description is arguably trite when considering that the moths were physically pinned to the boards with steel needles. Yet it was the liberation that arises when something is merely acknowledged as existing or having had existed: the busy life of objects left but not forgotten. The moths were fluttering, aware of the limited parameters of their happiness, having been brutally murdered with various chemicals, contortioned into the most unnatural positions – for such introverted insects – and then impaled upon a piece of board for the pleasure and knowledge of others.

The house began to feel different, in that Phyllis Ewans' personality and my own were becoming separate in what seemed the first time for many years. The clues of her past life still sat on the mantelpiece, the four photos – or technically three, if the idea that one is ripped into two is counted – staring down as I revelled in the idea of following the trail she had left for me. I considered that perhaps she had wanted me to know why she had hated her sister so much, and why she had been alone for so long, but I felt that I actually knew all of these things, but not in the way knowledge typically works through experience. It seemed that physical experience, that learning about the truth of Phyllis Ewans in an indisputable way, would be the key to unlock this realisation, even if the ghost of the knowledge haunted and spoke through the white noise of modern life.

I took this as further proof, with much relief at the time, that I was not actually a shard or fragment of her but very much myself, my own being. We had just slipped through each other at some point. There would be a time, so I thought, when I would look back upon this long period in my life with arrogant glee at having conquered it, having gained a reputation for supplying what was possibly the most interesting collection of Lepidoptera to the university department, and even having gained a house in a desirable area of London. All through simply surviving the torture of believing that I was someone else, now meeting themselves in some circular nightmare conceived as a punishment by forces unknown;. I could not wait for such a time of freedom to be upon me, when I could get back to work on the study of moths. I would no longer be considered ill or met with worried looks and glances from colleagues. On the contrary, I would be respected, and would have earned that respect through the work done with this vast collection of mounted moths.

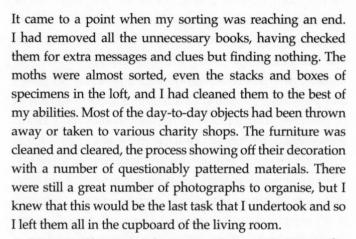

It came to a point when my sorting was reaching an end. I had removed all the unnecessary books, having checked them for extra messages and clues but finding nothing. The moths were almost sorted, even the stacks and boxes of specimens in the loft, and I had cleaned them to the best of my abilities. Most of the day-to-day objects had been thrown away or taken to various charity shops. The furniture was cleaned and cleared, the process showing off their decoration with a number of questionably patterned materials. There were still a great number of photographs to organise, but I knew that this would be the last task that I undertook and so I left them all in the cupboard of the living room.

It occurred to me after some days of finalising the cleaning that one thing I had not done, or even considered up to that point, was the hellish task of organising the things hanging on the walls, which were possibly the dirtiest items in the house. I removed the many framed objects into various bags, adding the moths to the room upstairs, which was now brimming with cleaned specimens in beautiful wooden frames. Walking out into the hallway when the task was largely complete, I realised that the only object now left hanging was the poplar hawk moth that had sparked my interest so many years previous.

I stared at the moth on the bare wall for a while – for a longer time than I can recall, as if time stood still in the presence of this insect. It stood out as a rare and beautiful object, the wall around it stained with the imprint of the missing objects that had crowded around. I began to think of the options for this

moth. I could have quite happily put it upstairs after cleaning
the thick layer of dust off the glass. But then I thought of how
common poplar hawk moths still were, and put the idea out
of my head, thinking that if it were gifted to the department
with the other specimens it would disappear and never be
properly appreciated. I decided to clean the framed mount
and then hang it back up as a personal memento. It was to
be 'kept for prosperity', so the phrase goes. I took the moth
from the wall, leaving the bare patch of wallpaper behind it,
fresh and unwearied by the many hours of sunlight suffered
through the window above the door.

I scraped away a line of dust from the glass to reveal the
moth inside. It had faded too, its lower left wing detached
almost entirely and now disintegrating at the bottom of
the frame. Something struck me about the moth that I had
not noticed before. The back of the frame was unusual,
and different from almost every other specimen. It seemed
thicker than when I had seen it hanging on the wall of the
house. I turned the moth around delicately and noticed
that the backing to the mount was quite loose, which
was unusual for Phyllis Ewans, who had been so precise
in regards to her mounting. 'There is nothing worse than
a loose and shoddy mount,' she had told me on various
occasions. I slowly picked away at the wood and card until
it became clear that there was something else behind it,
almost as if it had a second mount.

With surprising ease, this primary backing came away
entirely to reveal a secondary backing. On this card was
scrawled some writing that I knew was not Phyllis Ewans',

as I had seen so much of her handwriting in documents, notes and postcards. The primary backing had preserved the writing perfectly, its ink seeming as fresh as when it was first written. The text simply read, 'To my love, Phyl, thinking of you, Elsa', along with the date. The words sent shockwaves down my spine and I remember feeling faint once more. The sound of moths rose from nowhere, cacophonic and deafening. The moth fell out of my hands, the glass smashing on the hallway floor as the sound enveloped the space. The essence of Phyllis Ewans watched on from upstairs with hollowed eyes and stretched skin, seeming to grin as she appeared on the landing and drifted down towards me. I collapsed onto the floor, unable to take the sound of the hordes of moths, fluttering once more, unseen through the hallway.

5

I was now at the mercy of Phyllis Ewans. I no longer thought of our relationship as an obsession but as an illness. I needed to finalise the obsession in order to cure myself of this illness. The poplar hawk moth had given me the final piece of information that I needed, though the name Elsa had meant very little to me initially. Neither Phyllis Ewans nor her sister had ever mentioned the name. It could not have been the woman at her funeral, as she did not look like the woman in the photographs that I had found in the books; it was a given that Elsa was the woman in the photographs. The shattered hawk moth lay on the floor of the hallway for several days after I had dropped it. Its body became shockingly inconsequential in comparison to the mounting card on which it had been impaled.

I remember not moving for what felt like days, staring at the card and only performing the minimal basics of a living creature. The letters of the name, so I thought, must somehow reveal the secrets that I had been after. But

nothing gave way and the obsessive phase, built mostly
of staring at the writing for hours, broke down when the
pangs of a painful hunger jolted my body into action. The
mounting card was put in the middle of the mantelpiece
above the fireplace, bookended by the photographs, and I
went in search of food, recovering gradually as the days
passed. When finally in a fit state to consider my options,
I thought instantly of turning to Phyllis Ewans' many
address books, which had been used to blindly send out
her funeral invitations. In my haste to conquer the presence
in the house, I had tidied all such objects away. Yet I could
not, at that point, remember where I had moved them to.

The thought that, in my arrogance, I had thrown
them away filled me with a cold dread, a feeling that
was accompanied by the mocking, constant fluttering of
several moths behind my head. I would turn in anger, yet
they would be gone in an instant. The mocking insects
were at their worst during this period, as such discoveries
were inevitably disturbing the watching spirit of Phyllis
Ewans. I sensed her leaning over the hallway banister as
I walked from room to room downstairs, often looking up
and expecting to see her white, deathly face staring down
in teasing menace. But she would never show herself fully.
She was deceased; it was the illness of Phyllis Ewans that
really led to such feelings.

If I could have continued my investigation from outside
her house then I would have done so. The collage of her life,
however, needed to be picked apart there, even if it would
eventually lead me away from the city. I knew it would end

in the countryside of Wales. It was always to be Wales and the memories of the place. Her memories of the landscape regularly became one with my own in the dying moments before sleeping. The mysteries would be solved in those moments because they were our memories. I questioned, when lying on the duvet just before sleep, why I did not get up and write such memories down. My illness was briefly cured, and it could have been retained if only I could have got up off the bed and solidified them, the details of the life that she and I had somehow shared. Hers was an actual memory, mine a ghost memory. But all would slip away with sleep and dreams.

Eventually, I cleared up the shards of glass from the hallway that had once been the frame housing the poplar hawk moth. As the glass was flicked into a little plastic dustpan, I told myself that her address books had to still be in the house and that I had not thrown them out, making this point to myself as I tipped the shards into a bag. The little red books, which had seemed so inane and useless when I had looked at them initially, now seemed a sort of treasure. The house once again became a mess as the chaos began of going back through every surviving item that I had sorted. Dust that had settled in a relaxed fashion once more became swirling and airborne.

It mattered little that Phyllis Ewans was dead. Her presence was still around me, perhaps even inside me. My excavations into the arranged clutter began in haste, working in the same manner, beginning from the top bedroom. There was no sign of the books, and I felt that it was a waste of time looking in this room. I had bought some flowers for the desk mere days before, in my few hours of peace, with the strictest of intentions to keep them alive. They had already wilted and the petals, once a vibrant white, had quickly turned a deathly brown. It acted perfectly as a reflection of myself, of my own illness and my own possession by Miss Ewans. She would always be 'Miss' henceforth. That was an absolute certainty in my mind. But, as my illness required the methodical repetition of behaviour to know fully that the address books of Miss Ewans were not in every specific room, I needed to search thoroughly even if the action was an empty compulsion rather than a necessity.

My gut feeling was that they were downstairs in one of the cupboards. I chuckled rather ironically to myself as I rummaged manically through wardrobes and under the bed, almost enjoying what could now be described as my mania, a continuing gift from Miss Ewans and her dusty ghost. I was stretched out under the bed, my arms aching with the movement required to reach the very back, when I swore that the mattress above began to press downwards in a fashion that could only be caused by someone lying on top of it. The fluttering came once again, though as always, I could not see the moths. I wagered that they were a hawk moth of some sort, and survived the panicked moment by deceiving myself that the sound above could be caused by a rare hawk moth of some interest. But the pressure continued and I shouted out from my feeble position under the bed. I imagined what I must look like and how pathetic

I must seem, shouting at someone along with their ghostly moths, whilst trapped under a bed looking for something that I really knew to be downstairs in one of the cupboards.

This was the trapping of an obsessive compulsion, locked into an order that could not be broken. The fluttering once more faded into my perception. The name of Elsa came to taunt me in the air, travelling along the floating scales of dead wings. I swore one floated directly before my eyes, a shining pink and jet-black design suggesting it to be that of a decayed cinnabar moth. I allowed it a brief diversion into my memory of ragwort, of the puss moth caterpillar that had turned violently into a black wasp. I felt cocooned in my wooden crevasse, something devouring me from inside my memory. The act of remembering, so I thought, is the parasite of our hopes. It is parasitic. It lives and thrives upon us, whilst we live with the delusion that we define it, when it really defines us. It hatches, it devours and it destroys us from the inside out, until it is done and moves on to annihilate another life. I decided there and then that I was not going to let this parasite devour me, considering further that this was not even the parasite of my own memory, but doubly parasitic because it was the plague of someone else's memory.

In my final moment of despair, it came to me suddenly that a shock to my body was the only way to escape the routine of the obsession compulsion. I could see Miss Ewans' body floating towards me from the other room, the skin stretched back across her face, grinning with an eyeless smile, drifting slowly closer. With a last burst of energy, I shuffled into the hallway towards the top of the stairs from the bedroom. The top stair edged closer with each shuffle, a cacophony of moths behind me, taunting my efforts. But I had gravity on my side and, with one final movement, I fell off the top step and tumbled violently down. My plan had worked, for I was free from the cycle that my illness had trapped me in. Even if my body was now bruised from the fall, I knew that I could slowly make my way to where I believed the address book to be.

Lying on the floor, which still had minute shards of glass sticking out, I noticed a picture I had kept of Miss Ewans on the wooden cabinet in the hallway. I liked this picture as she had seemed rather content, sat in a rural garden holding a cat and in the company of a little black dog. But, I began to wonder, lying there on the carpet in the hallway in pain, whose garden was it? Now thinking more clearly after my fall, it was clearly the same garden and house in the hidden photograph that had been torn in two. The garden was from a different angle, but it was undoubtedly the same building. My own diminished perception over the previous weeks became abundantly clear: how had I not noticed this? Perhaps Miss Ewans had been on a walk or had captured several moths before the photo was taken, accounting for her happy disposition. All of this was masking a thought that had been dwelling in the recesses of my mind for some time: that, in spite of still being plagued by Miss Ewans – even going so far as to refer to her as my illness – I truly missed her. The photo seemed from another age, the colours mixed with a strange, red tint, even rendering the purple flowers in the garden dreamlike within a maroon haze.

Staring at the photo, my hands automatically began to check my body for injury, but there was only a slight ache from my side initially. The red reminded me of why I had thrown myself down the staircase: to save time in finding the little red address books that would lead me to Elsa, whoever Elsa may have been. Then it further struck me that this was, in all probability, Elsa's garden; that Miss Ewans was sitting in Elsa's garden, holding Elsa's cat. 'Don't let the dog stray too far, Phyl…' spoke a voice from our shared memory. The house was Elsa's or, so I assumed, was connected to her in some way. I lumbered up, keeping a close eye on the photograph in case some change occurred in my perception of it. Looking down, I felt as if I had only now taken it on board, perhaps for the first time since placing it in the hallway, which I only vaguely remembered doing.

All feeling returned and the fluttering of moths seemed far away in my mind. Making my way to the cabinet that I believed to hold the address books, my illness also seemed to dissipate. I was the strongest I had felt in some time, and I found the book with embarrassingly little effort. It made the action of throwing my body down the stairs seem even more manic in hindsight than it already was, but I also considered that it might have been some help to have done it more often. The book I needed seemed innocuous. I crouched down, my movements slow with the growing pain of something in my back beginning to bruise, and I began to flick through the books of names, addresses and phone numbers.

I admired Miss Ewans' detail within the address books, and the pages were filled with ephemera and typical tangents into her thoughts on walking and moths. I noticed that Miss Ewans had annotated the details of particular people with personal reflections, perhaps even reminders for herself as to why she avoided such people. The pages drifted past my fingers, sometimes stopping to ponder on the little notes about moths hidden in the corners. Miss Ewans had never really stopped in her research of Lepidoptera. I felt a slight shame wash over me with this realisation as, unlike Miss Ewans, my research had stopped completely.

Finally, with a flick of the address book, the name Elsa appeared. It had her details, including an address and phone number, but unusually, it was the only page I noticed without any scribbles, notes, annotations or ephemera of any kind. It was clear and unmarked which, to an untrained eye, might have seemed perfectly normal. Knowing Miss Ewans' almost constant need of some expression of her character and interests, it made it seem even more unusual.

A brief flutter went by behind my ear, a garden tiger probably, but I had completed my task. I had now found a contact who would be able to tell me more: the woman at the graveside, possibly. I was not going to wait for another attack from some similar vision of engulfing hordes of moths, and decided to call the number that went with the name immediately. The address was for a cottage in North Wales, not far from Snowdon. In fact, I was certain that I had been in the area where the cottage resided on one of my earliest walks. I had to reconnect the phone, having pulled out the cord at the very beginning of my endeavour. It was an old phone, the plastic having faded like the photographs and memories that lay all around the room. I decided that it would be best to sit down in order to speak to Elsa, and I placed the book on my lap so that there could be no mistake at all in dialling the number.

I had had so little contact with people for so long that, as the dial tone rang, I felt instantly and terribly worried. What if, so I thought, communication was now beyond me? What if, during the phone call, a sudden attack of moths distracted me and caused the caller to hang up or assume that I was, as they say, 'pulling their tail'. Or, even worse in my considerations, what if Elsa had moved from the house to somewhere else or was now even dead herself? With a disturbing agility, I envisioned thoughts of an arduous search for Elsa, stemming from information that I would have to beg for from the current occupiers of this house in Snowdonia and possibly many others. The call was picked up and a woman spoke.

I instantly fluffed my opening, forgetting to say hello and introduce myself, simply and abruptly asking, 'Is that Elsa?' The voice on the other end was at first flustered by my accidental abruptness, but quickly recovered, because it was obviously a relatively normal person. 'I'm afraid Elsa passed away some time ago, who is it please?' the voice said. I explained my position, being the friend and sole inheritor of Phyllis Ewans' property. The woman on the other end instantly acknowledged the connection and I felt relieved.

The moths would not be around any more today, I thought naively. I explained, somewhat falsely, that I was organising Miss Ewans' various objects and possessions and would need to discuss things in detail, with the potential of some inheritance coming her way. This was only false in the legal sense as, if the woman was to prove helpful, then

I would undoubtedly gift her something from the house, perhaps even the house itself. I further bolstered the story by explaining that my grandparents had dealt with Billie's estate, which was also entirely true though, with the tone of voice that I suggested it in, it probably hinted at a vast legal tradition in my family that belied the absurd reality of the situation. Mentioning Billie, however, did not have the effect that I desired.

Instead of aiding my story, it destabilised my negotiations with the woman on the phone whose name, I later learned, was Heather. As soon as I mentioned my grandparents' dealing with Billie, Heather's tone went perceivably colder than seconds before. It took some time to readjust my attitude to this new, colder persona, and I automatically began to sound more formal as a reaction. I needed to talk to her, even if she was uncomfortable with my association with Billie, of which there was actually very little.

I began to explain, almost pleadingly, that I had barely known her, having been very young in the last years of her life. This seemed to work, as Heather reverted to what I perceived to be a warmer reception to my inquiries. For a moment, I pondered how this woman had even known of Billie, considering whether I had unknowingly seen a picture of her when I had sorted through the photographs from her life some time ago. But this feeling quickly evolved into resentment; that, after all these years, Billie was still frustrating my understanding of her sister. Even from the grave, which the sisters admittedly now shared in some sense, she was hampering my investigations and,

ergo, hampering the cure for my illness. 'Well, I would be
very happy to meet you, Thomas, if you wanted to know
more about Elsa,' the woman said. I agreed that, as it was
down to me to communicate with Heather, I would make
the journey up to North Wales.

I arranged to travel to the house in Snowdonia, the
house that I assumed was the one I could see torn in two on
the mantelpiece. I wondered whether its plants would be
the same as in this photograph. I even wondered whether
I would recognise the village in which it sat, and whether
it would ignite other memories. It was organised and, with
the logistics of this permission finalised, I made to finish the
conversation so I could book the train tickets. But, in my
haste, I had forgotten to ask who Heather actually was. I
had been talking to a stranger without even acknowledging
her status as a stranger, as if we were old friends, or perhaps
even relatives. I had to ask her and there was no subtle way
of doing so. 'Before I go,' I said in a horrifically English and
repressed manner typical of people from these isles, 'who
in fact are you?' The tone implied some legal requirement,
and I considered grabbing a pen to make audible scribbles
so that it would sound as if I was filling in some necessary
paperwork or document. 'Oh,' she said, 'I'm Elsa's
daughter.' The long pause, which was due to both of us,
was deeply uncomfortable, and the slight flutter of moths
returned as I made an awkward farewell and hung the
phone back on the receiver. Considering that Miss Ewans
had never spoken of her and had gone to great lengths to
keep her mother's existence a secret, I was surprised that

she had made it to the funeral. She was the woman who had stood at the graveside and she must have received one of my blind funeral invites.

I had agreed with Elsa to travel the following day to her cottage or, as I later found out, her mother's cottage, not wishing to waste any more time. As I sank deep into the armchair that sat parallel to the window, I both admired and felt dismayed at my ambition. London, I considered, is actually quite far from North Wales. In fact, it may as well have been on the other side of the world considering my exhausted condition. My bones ached from the fall and the pain ground between my joints when I thought of the logistical nightmare involved in getting to this cottage in North Wales.

It was a place notorious for its meagre public transport, where the train which travelled up Mount Snowdon was arguably the only public transport service that ran even vaguely on time. My mind wandered in this dazed lull to thoughts of moths once more, not to the moths that were the symptom of my illness but to the poplar hawk moth in particular. The key to the history of Miss Ewans had lain before my eyes ever since I had first met her. I had many fond memories of this moth. It was arguably the beginning of her passing on the Lepidoptera obsession to me, the memories and experiences with the moth standing out for many years hence.

The smell of poplar trees always accompanied such thoughts concerning the moth, the smell carrying a powerful nostalgia that I could never quite place or resist. Describing the smell has always been difficult and, on brief occasions of coming across it when in company, I have always struggled to point out to my companions which smell it is that I'm excited about. 'It smells,' so I once began to a distant acquaintance, 'like leaves, but if leaves from ordinary trees had a relaxing, seductive quality.' My companion on that occasion had looked puzzled, as I recall, and became even more confused when I suggested with enthusiasm that the smell of poplar leaves really smells 'like the past.' I could never fully convey the smell of poplar leaves or why they aroused in me such a childish excitement. Sometimes I would simply suggest that the smell reminded me of the moth, which indeed it did, but it was never specifically why it was such a pleasant aroma.

Sitting slouched in the armchair, I wished deeply that I did not have to make this journey to North Wales, but I told myself there was a possibility of coming across a poplar tree or two on my journey. In fact, so I began to lecture myself, I could go for some walks straight after I had visited Elsa's cottage and had filled in the blank spaces I so desperately needed to fill. Poplar trees – or the thought of poplar trees – were driving me to finally begin the process of preparing. I already knew roughly where I needed to go, for the village where Elsa's cottage resided was, with some surprise, near to the village with the graveyard I had visited many years previous.

I knew that I would have to catch a train at Euston to the town of Bangor – or Gwynedd, as it is known in Welsh – then catch a bus to a nearby village from which I could then walk the rest of the way. Luckily, Miss Ewans had kept several Ordnance Survey maps of the area. I remembered an earlier moment of excitement: the possibility that some annotation on her maps could lead to further clues surrounding her life. I was wrong, and my mistake came back to me as I traced the long country road that Elsa's house sits in the middle of, finding the marker acknowledging the house and accepting that Miss Ewans had done nothing at all to highlight it. I was not worried by this, for the many clues she had left me up to that point had been enough to confirm my suspicions as just, and not simply the paranoia of a young man suffering from an illness of Miss Ewans.

My journey to North Wales was both the cure to my illness and even, perhaps, an exorcism of the house and everything around me. I would, in my new, healthy life, present Miss Ewans' collection of exquisite moths to the department. I would have the comfort and security of my job back and, most of all, I could continue once more with my own research. In the meantime, my journey to the cottage in North Wales was tedious, heightened by the inevitable delays to the trains and buses, and by the aching of my body, which I started to suspect was genuinely damaged by my fall down the stairs, rather than simply bruised. In my pockets, for I travelled naively light, I had brought the photographs found in Miss Ewans' books, along with the card that the poplar hawk moth had been mounted on. Alongside this was the OS map, simply as a precaution, and some bits of food that I had picked up from a shop in Euston Station. It occurred to me at that point that I could not remember the last time I had eaten, and I certainly did not have the option to prepare food for my journey.

Time was finally the last delusion in the illness of Miss
Ewans; which was my illness. Her illness, so I ultimately
accepted, had at most been a severe case of age, but time was
now a blur, not just on my journey but for what had seemingly
been several very long years. Whilst sat in the train during
the journey, I considered that I could no longer remember
what I had done the previous evening, after I had called
Heather. I could not remember packing my meagre array of
paraphernalia, and I could not remember debating what else
to bring with me, or even the moment of falling asleep.

I had blinked for a few instances after the phone call to
Heather and had found myself straight at Euston Station, ready
for the trip. My body had been aching for each leg of the journey,
a feeling of dismay permeating just before each moment that
required my movement. I must go and seek medical attention
when the opportunity occurs, I thought, as a particularly bad
pothole in the road jolted the chassis of my Welsh bus, sending a
spasm of pain down my spine. I distracted myself with thoughts
of my earlier ventures around this landscape, imagining the
wonderful specimens I had caught in the forests and fields all
around, though it could not fully remove the pain.

Eventually the bus came to the stop that I recognised
as mine. It wasn't really in the village that I had assumed
but was on the very outskirts of that village, those first
few ephemeral houses signalling to people approaching
that they are nearing civilisation, and signalling to people
leaving that they are departing civilisation. The bus drove
away and I hobbled to the other side of the road, frustration
growing as there was obviously no pavement to walk on.

I considered myself, walking down a long country road away from civilisation towards the middle of nowhere. And worst of all, I was going out of necessity rather than for something worthwhile, such as the search for an interesting specimen or for the enjoyment of a good walk. I opted to climb slowly over a slate wall that led to an adjacent field used for grazing sheep and to walk among the grass rather than face the cars. Perhaps there were ticks hidden in the greenery, but I would rather face them than the continued pain caused by the hard tarmac.

The journey continued, and I hoped more and more to see the large house from the photographs on the horizon, a sense of worry beginning to grow as the map had clearly diminished the reality of the road's length, which was several miles long. It was only when finally following the turn of an uphill bend that a house came into a view, the house that had been quietly in my memories for so long. The garden of the house, which I referred to as the Welsh House, was even more splendid and grand than the pictures had originally conveyed. Slowly and painfully clambering back over the slate wall – for I did not want to make a bad impression by simply wandering around the rear from an adjacent field – I took my time in admiring the many plants which stood on the slopes of the front garden, slightly hunched over with pain. The views from the back, so I thought, must have been beautiful down into the valley, which I assumed wound on behind, forever.

The garden patio was neat and tidy, nothing like the messy gardens that Miss Ewans herself had ever attempted to look after. She was a keen believer in 'benign neglect', as she would always call it, and insisted that the scrubby potential of weeds was better for the caterpillars and, therefore, better for the moths. With a garden as grand as this, I thought, such benign neglect would be largely unnecessary, for the countryside all around would provide moths aplenty. I made my way up the path that trickled through the lawn and under a wide porch to the front door. I became steadily nervous, consciously aware that my body was reducing my steps to an embarrassingly slow pace. The bell jangled from inside and Heather came to the door. The moment was one of brief relief as I instantly recognised her from Miss Ewans' funeral; her shoulders sank heavily down onto her body with a melancholy that was instantly recognisable.

She welcomed me in, but I could not in that moment move. I had been ignoring the brief flutters behind my head whilst walking down the long valley road. Heather asked if I was all right and, clearly sensing that I was not, held my arm as she led me in. I was frustrated with myself for letting such phantom Lepidoptera spoil what was meant to be a defining moment. I tried in vain to take note of all the items around me on the walls, noticing finally that there were some mounts of moths there, though the house did not possess the same atmosphere comprised of scales and wings as Miss Ewans' house did. Heather sat me down on a large couch residing in an incredibly sunny room, and I noticed the view from the wide conservatory windows behind the house. I was correct: the view out over the valley was stunning.

Heather sat down opposite me and I noticed how much older she looked now that I could see her properly. The moths had gone and I believed, naively, that I was about to banish them permanently, curing my illness. 'I inherited this house from my mother,' she said as she stirred tea in a twee china cup; the insufferable politeness of repetition. She asked how I knew Miss Ewans, even though I had given her several details in our phone conversation. I suggested to her finally that I was after information regarding her mother and that, despite being the sole heir of the estate, I would be quite willing to gift some of it to anyone who could prove to have played a significant part in Miss Ewans' life. I was incredibly proud of this wording because it sounded very legal, and it hid my now storming mania behind a veil of calm bureaucracy. And then she began to talk, rendering me silent as I waited patiently for the antidote to be applied.

'My mother and Phyllis worked in the same department for some time many years ago. You probably saw the moths on the wall,' she said. I briefly took this as a slight, but then remembered which moths she was referring to and assumed quite rightly that she could not see the horde circling behind me, fluttering away as memories do. 'But I actually think Mother met her whilst walking one day further down the valley. I imagine the meeting of two entomologists in such an obscure place – and female entomologists in those days, to boot – took them both rather by surprise.' She paused and moved to a bureau which, from glancing in the drawer, was clearly brimming with photographs. She pulled out a handful from an envelope and came back to sit opposite. I was trying to hide my impatience and my keenness to know more, but I held myself back, sitting in perfect silence. Heather put a photo of the house on the table in front of me and I recognised it immediately. It was a similar photo to the torn-up Polaroid that Miss Ewans had hidden in the books, but with a few subtle differences.

Unlike in Miss Ewans' version, the sky was a more faded blue and the angle closer to the house. They were undoubtedly taken together, as if shared between the two women. I put the photo back on the table and Heather continued. 'This was the house several years ago. Phyllis would come here whenever she was walking the hills and the mountains, or whenever she was in the area really. She didn't especially get on with my father, however, who was in business and was never really here. I knew from an early age that my mother and father were merely playing at being the loving couple, to provide me with a stable childhood. But I suppose this has little to do with Phyllis, or Billie for that matter.' She skirted off the subject and began to look through the photos, which I assumed she had brought out as evidence for my legal farce.

'My mother was not the most adept lepidopterist in the world, and there were great gaps in her knowledge that made work very hard, especially in those days when Lepidoptera was chiefly a field for men.' She could see that the realisation was not lost upon me, having already told her on the phone, albeit by sheer accident, that I had some knowledge in the field of moths. I admitted this during the conversation, as it was all too clear that my ploy of creating the pretence of some legal errand was impossible to maintain. 'A lot of these photographs here were actually taken by Phyllis. She always used to carry a variety of cameras later in life that printed out the photos there and then. She would give copies to my mother as a gift, even after they stopped meeting regularly. Phyllis could be incredibly generous when she wanted to be, though I remember that she did her utmost to avoid me.'

I could believe both of these things quite easily as Miss Ewans had always had a certain aversion to children, and I had also found an array of different cameras in her loft during my first intensive attempt at organising her house. 'The university that both Phyllis and my mother worked in was incredibly underfunded, and there was always a great worry that it was going to close, especially when funding was so desperately needed elsewhere in those

days. It was actually Phyllis who helped get my mother
the job in the department, arguing for her merits when she
had initially failed her interview with the department
because of nervousness.' Heather began to flick through
the photographs again, pointing out several which Miss
Ewans had taken on her many visits to the Welsh House.
One photograph perfectly captured the beauty of the view
from the back garden.

The picture had aged well, with the colours devoid of that typical reddish hue that I had seen in others she had taken. Everything about it suggested the potential for moths, an eye for landscape that potentially held a great number of specimens. I could follow her logic and the way it worked just from the photograph, briefly falling into a memory once more that suggested that I myself had taken the photograph. I could picture looking down at my feet and seeing the paving of the garden, in between checking the view of the valley. I took the object in the picture to be a sundial but, wandering in the memory – our memory – I could see that it was actually a birdbath. I inadvertently looked away from Heather and into the garden to check that I was correct, but I could not see the paved area. 'Where has the birdbath gone?' I asked. Heather confirmed to me that it had broken a long time ago and was never replaced.

She could see that she had lost me again, though she was clearly unaware that it was memories that were taking my attention rather than some sort of boredom. Everything in her eyes suggested that she was dealing with a bored person, rather than a person deeply reliving everything she had presented. 'I'm glad Phyllis took all of these random pictures, for my mother didn't especially like taking photographs. She was almost suspicious of such things but Phyllis would insist on preserving the moments for a later occasion.'

'Such as this,' I blurted out loud and Heather nodded, though I regretted the outburst. I could feel myself nearing some truth, but it would take more effort on my part. I mentioned how I had met Miss Ewans and how Billie had made an initial impression on me in those years. The mention of Billie put a stop to Heather's initial openness in talking about her mother for a time, and so I attempted to claw back the trust I had built up.

My eyes wandered around the room, looking for some object that I could use to change the subject. There were only a handful of moths on the walls and they were not well mounted or preserved. I could judge this even without closer inspection, and I began to feel uncomfortable with my own body language, fluctuating between a mixture of damning critic and manic ruin. I could not avoid the fluttering gathering once more and saw the dead scales of moth wings float gradually down at the corner of my eyes, the light from the sun highlighting the dust and the scales in equal measure, like snowfall that had followed me indoors. I found a brief respite in the form of a grandfather clock, my desired object to break the awkward silence that grew between us. I pointed nervously to the object, noting the craftsmanship that had gone into it. 'I've seen the instructions on how to fix that very clock,' I said to Heather, with that desperate optimism of someone in the process of falling apart. 'The instructions for the mechanism,' I continued, 'were kept on a piece of card that Miss Ewans kept around her house. To fix it is a surprisingly simple operation,' the words continued to tumble out. I noticed that the legal language I had initially desired to speak with kept reasserting itself, making everything I said sound even more awkward and unhinged than it already was.

'Yes, it's a very nice clock. My mother inherited it from

her mother and I think it goes back a number of generations. I don't remember Phyllis taking much notice of it at the time but, as I say, she avoided me.' She began to tail off again, but I was not going to let this strand die as I did before. I was going to plumb its depths for all it was worth, considering that this was probably the only time I was going to speak to this woman. I had, so I thought, very little to lose, so I began to ask about what Miss Ewans did on her visits to the Welsh House and why she had never mentioned Elsa to me. Heather did not speak for some time, and so, to keep the momentum going, I began to recall various occasions from the previous years.

I told her of my time looking after Miss Ewans in the later days of her life, the many visits to houses, gardens and reserves that I took her on, and how I had put my life on hold to organise and sort through her possessions, including her excellent collection of moths. I told the complete truth regarding my actual work, that of a lepidopterist – an interest spiked by Miss Ewans– and how we had seen each other at her funeral. Heather could see that I was not willing to accept mere shards of answers, hints at what she was really discussing but, so I thought with a gradually biting worry, I could see that I was not going to get all of the information I was after.

Or, perhaps, the information that I desperately needed Heather to say, fully and out loud, would be left assumed. My illness of Miss Ewans would continue, if such a thing were possible. I needed her to say the words, and I needed her to spell it out. But the conversation continued, driven by useless bits of information. 'These moths,' I began to relate to Heather, 'have been painstakingly organised and sorted, and, though

there is still some work to do on finalising the collection, I am
going to gift them to the university department. However,'
I said, 'I can only do so once Miss Ewans' estate is in proper
order.' I presented so many opportunities for Heather to say
what really happened with Miss Ewans, with her mother and
with Billie, but it seemed impossible. Heather began to fill in
more trivial gaps with help from the photographs from the pile.
The first was a pleasing surprise, in that it was identical to the
picture I had found in one of the books, of Elsa stood by the
large Welsh lake that I had fallen into visions of when in the
woodland as a teenager. But in this photo, the subject was now
Miss Ewans herself, standing on the same jetty. The photos had
been conceived as a pair, to share a memory that both women
desired to be recorded. I could hear the water once more but,
in my lapse of perception, I was now looking away from the
lake, the splashes of water coming from behind. I could see the
female photographer who I now knew to be Elsa, and felt a
glow of affection and sadness.

'That trip,' Heather continued, 'was many years after the
period when they were good friends, a sort of reunion. It
was such a shame.' Heather knew there was more to say, and
I considered the feeling of melancholy that I was deriving
from falling into the memory of the photograph. It was many
years later, but from what? I still could not persuade Heather
to say anything out loud. 'It was a trip to their favourite
landscape not all that far from here, and I remember that
my mother was surprised at how cosmopolitan Phyl then
seemed, with her lavish coats in particular.'

I hadn't considered this aspect, and noted that, contrary

to her consistent ramshackle appearance as a scientist, Miss Ewans looked dressed up in these photographs. I had been too busy seeing through her eyes to notice that she had clearly gone to some effort, at least more effort than usual. Another photo was dropped onto the table, this time of the old hotel with the vine leaves growing up the walls and over the slate roof. It was the hotel where they had stayed on that same trip, and I barely recognised Miss Ewans. Her whole demeanour was cosmopolitan yet again. I had sorted through all of her clothing and had found nothing remotely like the coat she was wearing. She had lived a secret life, one which her ghostly memory had contrived to torment me with. But I still felt no closer to an escape from the compulsions driven by my parasitic memories.

I no longer wanted to be confused about who I was. I wanted to be Thomas, and for her to definitely be Phyllis Ewans. The line between us was far from the solid divide that I had hoped coming here would confirm. It actually seemed that it would become worse, the moths fluttering more and more as my hope of returning to work, to the study of Lepidoptera, diminished into the air thick with scales. My main fear was of becoming Miss Ewans, disappearing entirely into her memories with my own falling away. I could see the hotel so clearly, more clearly than in the photograph, and I could feel the uneven paving that led to the hotel's entrance under my feet, grateful that I was wearing sensible shoes.

I was myself then, and she was Miss Ewans: the melancholic

woman somehow spited by her sister. Heather had virtually vanished from my thoughts by the time I re-entered the room. Luckily, with my disposition being so incredibly awkward, the silence that ensued seemed a perfectly natural occurrence. Of course, so I imagined Heather thinking, he's not quite there: he's lived with Phyllis Ewans for long enough. Feeling my mind slipping away, I concluded that time was limited and that Heather had to help me escape from the moths and their dead-wing storms. Then, as I drank a mouthful of floral tea, a thought occurred. I would upset her, I thought, by suggesting how wonderful Billie had been when younger, how I wished I could have known her more.

I began my ploy, recalling the photos I had found of Billie in the house in Cheshire, referencing her delight in socialites and how, though I was lying, I wished Miss Ewans had been more like her. My ploy worked almost instantly, as Heather came to life with a jolt of memories, reacting to my words. 'What nonsense,' she said loudly and inadvertently. I could see the regret in her face, and the recognition of how I had achieved such a reaction. Then she sighed, a hopeful sign of defeat in this battle of silence. 'That woman lost my mother her job. That woman's...' she paused for a moment, considering her words carefully. 'That woman's meddling cost my mother her job. That woman was not "the life and soul of the party", as she had always carried on. She was a gossiper who cost my mother her job, almost cost Phyl hers and almost cost both of them a warning.' I could not quite believe what I was hearing and went to ask a question, but Heather continued. 'Things were different then. Phyl was lucky to keep her job, even if it meant becoming a virtual recluse.' But questions were forming in my mind and Heather still refused to say what I needed to be said, what I had known all along from the memories that I had shared. I just needed her to say it.

Hordes of pale eggars flew around the room, blending in with the dated decor, now even daring to fly before my eyes. Heather whispered to herself once more, 'Things were different then.' I began to accept that this would be it, that I was to be doomed forever to false memories of moths and confusion. For I knew, and had always known, the mysteries behind the life of Miss Ewans. They had lain in wait like the wasp's egg, sat in the heart of my body, ready to burst and devour at its own pleasure and pace. But I could accept that such an egg was there only if the confirmation was spoken out loud. Heather was to show me one final photograph. The Polaroid simply had the pair of women together, and I could see that Heather was hopeful that this would be enough, that nothing else would need to be said.

But the photograph was not enough; it could have meant anything. I envisioned my future life whilst looking at this photograph, wasting away in her house, unsure of who I was or how to deal with the visions that had tormented me since my teenage years. But then, looking once more around the living room of the Welsh House, with its pathetic furnishings and meagre display of poorly mounted moths, I gathered my energy for one last attempt. Heather clearly knew that nothing from Miss Ewans' estate was coming her way. She had, so to speak, nothing to lose. 'But what did Elsa mean to Miss Ewans?' I asked. The thought of direct questions had not come to mind during my walk to the Welsh House, as I had expected complete openness.

But I was wrong, and direct questions were all I had left to prevent the now raging horde of moths from forever engulfing my life. At first Heather did not acknowledge the question at all, using the excuse of pouring another cup of tea from the pot to avoid speaking. The liquid took an infinitely long time to flow into the cup, and this was clearly quite deliberate. She then sat back, staring straight at me, the spirit of Miss Ewans hanging above her with a hollow-eyed smile once again as the white noise of the moths drew ever closer, fragments of scales and dead wings slowly but confidently raining downwards in front of my eyes. Heather could not see them but I could, covering the floor and filling the room. She went to say something but then stopped in the most horrifically theatrical of ways. I paused for breath, the shock of being taken to the precipice causing my whole body to slump and deflate. My hand reached for the piece of card on which the poplar hawk moth had been mounted, almost slamming it down on the table so that Heather could read the inscription, the words that I had hoped would force her hand. I could not take another moment of this torture, and blurted out another direct question. 'What did Miss Ewans do?' I said with a manic disposition, my hands shaking as I drowned in the cacophony of moth wings. Heather looked up, the Lepidoptera now torrential in the permanent downpour that I became forever trapped within. 'Phyllis Ewans walked,' she said, 'and that is all.'

"The moth having righted himself now lay most decently and uncomplainingly composed. O yes, he seemed to say, death is stronger than I am."

— Virginia Woolf, 'The Death of the Moth' (1942)

Acknowledgements

My thanks must firstly go to my Nan and to the real "Phyllis" whose photographs were used in this book. I was lucky enough to know Phyllis for much of her long life and being gifted her photos after she had passed away was a defining moment in deciding how I was going to write my fiction. My heartfelt gratitude to my grandmother especially for preserving the photos and for the many real and happy memories we shared of Phyllis.

Thanks to my parents, Jan and Keith, for their ever constant support. In particular, thanks to my father for imbuing in me an interest in moths at an early age which has never left.

My utmost thanks to Gary Budden and Kit Caless at Influx Press who gave me faith in both this book and my own writing, at a time when it was at its lowest and had been thoroughly beaten to a bloody pulp. Thanks to Dan

Coxon for his great editing job and Vince Haig for the wonderful cover art and design.

Thanks in particular must go to Max Porter at Granta whose advice in the initial stages of editing my first draft was invaluable and dramatically changed this book for the better.

My thanks to Harriet Thorpe for the loan of "Baby Blue" in the scanning and editing of the original photos. I am still "following the water."

My general thanks to those who continue to support and help with my work – in writing, in film and elsewhere – that includes: John Atkinson, Jeff Barrett, Ramsey Campbell, Tom Killingbeck, Dr Robert Macfarlane, Andrew Male, Andy Miller, Leah Moore, Benjamin Myers, Gareth E. Rees, John Reppion, Ellen Rogers, Dr Holly Rogers, John Rogers, David Southwell, Simon Spanton, Luke Turner, Nick Ware, Paul Watson, my friends at the Folk Horror Revival, my friends at the British Film Institute and many, many others.

My final thanks to Caroline who helped me stay vaguely sane during the writing of this book. My memories of reading the manuscript with you in the garden in Truchtersheim is one I will always treasure.

About the Author

Adam Scovell is a writer and filmmaker from Merseyside now based in London. His writing has featured in *The Times*, BFI, *Sight & Sound*, *Little White Lies* and *The Quietus*. He runs the website, *Celluloid Wicker Man*, and his film work has been screened at a variety of festivals and events. In 2015, he worked with Robert Macfarlane on an adaptation of his *Sunday Times* best-seller, *Holloway*, and has worked on films alongside Stanley Donwood, Iain Sinclair and BAFTA-nominated director, Paul Wright. His first book, *Folk Horror: Hours Dreadful and Things Strange*, was published by Auteur in 2017 and he has recently completed his PhD at Goldsmiths University.

INFLUX
PRESS

Influx Press is an independent publisher based in London, committed to publishing innovative and challenging fiction, poetry and creative non-fiction from across the UK and beyond. Formed in 2012, we have published titles ranging from award-nominated fiction debuts and site-specific anthologies to squatting memoirs and radical poetry.

www.influxpress.com
www.patreon.com/InfluxPress
@Influxpress

THE STONE TIDE:
ADVENTURES AT THE END OF THE WORLD
Gareth E. Rees

'Simultaneously quotidian and grotesque, *The Stone Tide* is the funniest, most readable, most intelligently self-searching book I've read in years.'
— M John Harrison, author of *Light*

'The problems started the day we moved to Hastings…'

When Gareth E. Rees moves to a dilapidated Victorian house in Hastings he begins to piece together an occult puzzle connecting Aleister Crowley, John Logie Baird and the Piltdown Man hoaxer. As freak storms and tidal surges ravage the coast, Rees is beset by memories of his best friend's tragic death in St Andrews twenty years earlier. Convinced that apocalypse approaches and his past is out to get him, Rees embarks on a journey away from his family, deep into history and to the very edge of the imagination. Tormented by possessed seagulls, mutant eels and unresolved guilt, how much of reality can he trust?

The Stone Tide is a novel about grief, loss, history and the imagination. It is about how people make the place and the place makes the person. Above all it is about the stories we tell to make sense of the world.

ISBN: 9781910312070

MARSHLAND:
DREAMS AND NIGHTMARES ON THE EDGE OF LONDON

Gareth E. Rees

'Whatever it is, New Weird, Cryptozoology, Psychogeography or Deep Map, *Marshland* is simply essential reading.'
— Caught by the River

'I had become a bit part in the dengue-fevered fantasy of a sick city.'

Cocker spaniel by his side, Gareth E. Rees wanders the marshes of Hackney, Leyton and Walthamstow, avoiding his family and the pressures of life. He discovers a lost world of Victorian filter plants, ancient grazing lands, dead toy factories and tidal rivers on the edgelands of a rapidly changing city.

Ghosts are his friends. As strange tales of bears, crocodiles, magic narrowboats and apocalyptic tribes begin to manifest themselves, Rees embarks on a psychedelic journey across time and into the dark heart of London.

Marshland is a deep map of the east London marshes, a blend of local history, folklore and weird fiction, where nothing is quite as it seems. Gareth E Rees has written a London text like no other.

ISBN: 9780957169395

HOW THE LIGHT GETS IN
Clare Fisher

'Cements her position as an innovative literary talent.'
— *New Statesman*

'Fisher's tales are funny and moving, and you'll treasure them all.'
— *Stylist*

'If fiction was a language, Clare Fisher would be one of its native speakers: a writer whose whole response to the world is brilliantly story-shaped.
— Francis Spufford

How The Light Gets In is the first collection from award winning short story writer and novelist, Clare Fisher. A book of very short stories that explores the spaces between light and dark and how we find our way from one to the other.

From buffering Skype chats and the truth about beards, to fried chicken shops and the things smartphones make you less likely to do when alone in a public place, Fisher paints a complex, funny and moving portrait of contemporary British life.

ISBN: 9781910312124

ATTRIB. AND OTHER STORIES
Eley Williams

WINNER OF THE JAMES TAIT BLACK PRIZE 2018

WINNER OF THE REPUBLIC OF CONSCIOUSNESS PRIZE 2018

'She is a writer for whom one struggles to find comparison, because she has arrived in a class of her own.'
— Sarah Perry, author of *The Essex Serpent*

It's just the real inexplicable gorgeous brilliant thing this book. I love it in a way I usually reserve for people.
— Max Porter, author of *Grief Is The Thing With Feathers*

Attrib. and other stories celebrates the tricksiness of language just as it confronts its limits. Correspondingly, the stories are littered with the physical ephemera of language: dictionaries, dog-eared pages, bookmarks and old coffee stains on older books. This is writing that centres on the weird, tender intricacies of the everyday where characters vie to 'own' their words, tell tall tales and attempt to define their worlds.

With affectionate, irreverent and playful prose, the inability to communicate exactly what we mean dominates this bold debut collection from one of Britain's most original new writers.

ISBN: 9781910312162

GHOSTS ON THE SHORE:
TRAVELS ALONG GERMANY'S BALTIC COAST
Paul Scraton

'A powerful story of human tragedy and its inheritances, of "the hubris of territorial ambition" – less a story of a landscape than of a shifting culture and people.'
— Times Literary Supplement

'Deeply immersive and richly braided.'
— Julian Hoffman, author of *The Small Heart of Things*

Inspired by his wife's collection of family photographs from the 1930s and her memories of growing up on the Baltic coast in the GDR, Paul Scraton set out to travel from Lübeck to the Polish border on the island of Usedom, an area central to the mythology of a nation and bearing the heavy legacy of trauma.

Exploring a world of socialist summer camps, Hanseatic trading towns long past their heyday and former fishing villages surrendered to tourism, Ghosts on the Shore unearths the stories, folklore and contradictions of the coast, where politics, history and personal memory merge to create a nuanced portrait of place.

ISBN: 9781910312100

BUILT ON SAND
Paul Scraton

'Paul Scraton should be encouraged to go on more long walks.'
— Hidden Europe

Berlin: long-celebrated as a city of artists and outcasts, but also a city of teachers and construction workers. A place of tourists and refugees, and the memories of those exiled and expelled. A city named after marshland; if you dig a hole, you'll soon hit sand.

The stories of Berlin are the stories *Built on Sand*. A wooden town, laid waste by the Thirty Years War that became the metropolis by the Spree that spread out and swallowed villages whole. The city of Rosa Luxemburg and Joseph Roth, of student movements and punks on both sides of the Wall. A place still bearing the scars of National Socialism and the divided city that emerged from the wreckage of war.

Built on Sand centres on the personal geographies of place, and how memory and history live on in the individual and collective imagination.

ISBN:9781910312339

AN UNRELIABLE GUIDE TO LONDON

'This is London, inglorious yet profound.'
— Never Imitate

An Unreliable Guide to London brings together twenty-three stories about the lesser known parts of a world renowned city. Stories that stretch the reader's definition of the truth and question reality. Stories of wind nymphs in South Clapham tube station, the horse sized swan at Brentford Ait, sleeping clinics in Islington and celebrations for St Margaret's Day of the Dead.

An Unreliable Guide to London is the perfect summer read for city dwellers up and down the country. With a list of contributors reflecting the multi-layered, complex social structures of the city, it is the guide to London, showing you everything that you never knew existed.

Authors:

M John Harrison; Chloe Aridjis; Gary Budden; Kit Caless; Yvvette Edwards; Courttia Newland; Will Wiles; Noo Saro-Wiwa; Nikesh Shukla; Juliet Jacques; Salena Godden; Stephen Thompson; Irenosen Okojie; Sunny Singh; Paul Ewen; Tim Burrows; George F.; Gareth E. Rees; Aki Schilz; Tim Wells; Koye Oyedeji; Eley Williams; Stephanie Victoire

ISBN:9781910312223

SIGNAL FAILURE:
LONDON TO BIRMINGHAM, HS2 ON FOOT
Tom Jeffreys

'Through it all, Jeffreys's writing is intelligent, engaging and engaged, and deeply and disarmingly human.'
— New Statesman

One November morning, Tom Jeffreys set off from Euston Station with a gnarled old walking stick in his hand and an overloaded rucksack. His aim was to walk the 119 miles from London to Birmingham along the proposed route of HS2. Needless to say, he failed.

Over the course of ten days of walking, Jeffreys meets conservationists and museum directors, fiery farmers and suicidal retirees. From a rapidly changing London, through interminable suburbia, and out into the English countryside, Jeffreys goes wild camping in Perivale, flees murderous horses in Oxfordshire, and gets lost in a landfill site in Buckinghamshire. *Signal Failure* weaves together poetry and politics, history, philosophy and personal observation to form an extended exploration of people and place, nature, society, and the future.

ISBN:9781910312148

BINDLESTIFF

Wayne Holloway

'A devastating vision of what America is becoming, wrapped up in a compelling and compassionate fable of what it is today.'
— Krishnan Guru-Murthy

'Hip, funny and aware, a sharp satire and phantasmagorical romp of almost obscenely impeccable reference..'
— Chris Petit, author of *Robinson*

2036. In a ramshackle, backwater United States, Marine Corp vet Frank Dubois journeys from L.A. to Detroit, seeking redemption for a life lived off the rails, in a country derailed from its own manifest destiny.

In present day Hollywood, a wannabe British film director hustles to get his movie 'Bindlestiff' off the ground starring 'Frank', a black Charlie Chaplin figure cast adrift in post-federal America.

Weaving together prose and screenplay *Bindlestiff* explores the power and responsibility of storytelling, revealing what lies behind the voices we read and the characters we see on screen. We open with a simple image of a man mending a hole in his shoe using a cut off piece of rubber and a tube of glue. From there the story explodes into a broiling satire on race, identity, family, friendship, war, peace, sex, drugs but precious little rock and roll.

ISBN: 9781910312292